THE SACRED
STRANGER

RON LEATH

For my mother, Jennifer Rainey.
Your strength, your wisdom, and your quiet sacrifices shaped me more than I can ever say.
I still hear your voice.
And in every page I write, I'm chasing the light you gave me.

This story is for you.

"Do not forget to show hospitality to strangers, for by so doing some people have shown hospitality to angels without knowing it"

—Hebrews 13:2

CHAPTER ONE

I couldn't think of any good reason to stop here.

But something about this town made my foot ease off the gas. I rolled through slow, scanning every house, every building, wondering what about this town had my attention.

Then a diner—gas station combo came into view. Nothing special, just the brightest thing I'd seen for miles.

Still, the feeling grew louder. It wasn't a thought. It was more like… an invitation. Maybe even God telling me to pull over.

Or maybe I was just tripping and needed some sleep.

I pulled into the gas station and parked toward the end. My gas light had come on a few miles back, so I'm not sure why I parked instead of pulling up to a pump. I told myself I'd fuel up after eating.

I checked the time. 6:05. Three hours down, six

more to go. I'd be in Jordan Heights just after midnight, giving me enough time to rest before sealing the most important deal of my career.

I'm Micah Peterson. Thirty-five. Been with my current company for twelve years. Made a few out of state moves for the company and now I reside in Dallas, Texas with my wife and two boys.

Each relocation was hard—new city, new friends, new roads…but every move came with a promotion. A better opportunity for me and my family.

And now my focus was on making it to Jordan Heights to close the biggest deal of my tenure. If things go as planned, maybe I'd get that final promotion… a spot on the board. I'd have to move to Chicago, but like they say, you gotta go where the money sends you.

But I'd even settle for Senior Executive—at least for now. I'd finally get that corner office overlooking Dallas skyline. A prime parking spot. Too many perks to name.

But this wasn't just about status and benefits… I'm a Christian. I cared about other things like legacy and security. Praising God while at the same time, creating wealth for me and my family.

That's why I didn't let a flight delay stop me from getting to Jordan Heights. Instead, I took the initiative and drove.

I owe it all to God. His timing. His favor. The way he positioned me. He's done great things for me, and this felt like the next one.

So, I think of this as walking into inheritance.

Doing what I'm supposed to do, the way I'm supposed to do it. Faith, strategy, and execution. Utilizing my God-given talent.

When my quiet praise ended, I stepped out of the car. The weight in the sky pressed down on my shoulders. The air was thick. Purple-gray clouds hung low, undecided on whether it wanted to storm or welcome in the dark.

Up close, the gas station still wasn't anything special. Old pumps. Flickering lights. The building itself looked like it hadn't changed at all since it was first built.

I walked inside. I gave a polite nod to the clerk at the register, then made my way to the diner section. It sat in the back corner, connected by design, but living in its own separate world.

I found a seat by the window. The glass was foggy. It didn't give much of a view, but I could make out a long stretch of darkening sky and the rough outline of hills in the distance.

Everything felt quiet. You could hear conversations. Every clink of silverware on porcelain. The type of environment I'm not used to in the hustle and bustle of Dallas.

I got a few stares but not the kind to make you feel unwelcome. Maybe just the curious, 'where's he from' vibe. Hard to not notice a tall, two hundred pound plus, black man showing up alone, in a small, secluded diner after dark.

But I smiled every time my eyes met with someone. There was nothing strange or out of the ordinary.

Until I saw *him*.

Far corner. Beige coat. Sitting still—a little too still.

Watching me. Not in a threatening way, more like curiosity. Or maybe even familiarity. I had a strange feeling that he was the one who'd drawn me to this place.

'Nah, I'm tripping,' I said to myself. Maybe I was just tired. When you push to stay awake, your mind starts playing games. And determination can cover up exhaustion, but it also makes you see things that aren't there… or twist what *is* there into something that's not.

I brushed it off. Made eye contact with the waitress as she chatted with the seemingly locals.

Once she saw me, she wrapped up her conversation and glided over to my table with a warm but tired smile. She held a carafe and poured the coffee without asking.

"Hey there," she said, voice a little raspy, like she'd been talking all day. "Just passing through?"

"Yes ma'am," I said, sliding the coffee closer to me. "I'm on my way to Jordan Heights. Stopped in for a quick bite then getting gas before I hit the road again."

She smiled—the kind you give when you've heard more than you asked for but too polite to admit.

She handed me a laminated menu. Small but fitting. This wasn't IHOP or Denny's. Just a little diner with seemingly good people and hopefully good food.

"Well, I'm glad you stopped in," she said. "I'll give you a few minutes to look the menu over. And just so you know, our special of the day is the deluxe cheeseburger. Two patties, all the fixings and bottomless fries for $6.99."

I looked down at the menu like I needed to see it to believe it. I could barely get a coffee for that price in Dallas.

The door chime rang, pulling her attention toward the entrance. An older gentleman walked in—worn flannel, gray beard, hands that had seen real work.

"Be right back to check on you," she said, walking over to him.

She sat him two tables in front of me, close enough that I could see and hear their exchange.

Leaning down, with her elbows on the table, she smiled. "I didn't expect to see you until next week sometime. You just can't get enough of this place, huh?"

He let out a rough chuckle, removing his hat. "I was actually about to drop off a load in Bethany Grove but turned around just before 287. Winds are too strong out there. Matter of fact, it's heading this way. Hope y'all close up on time tonight."

My eyes crinkled. I'd seen Bethany Grove on the map. It wasn't too far from Jordan Heights. And 287 was the final stretch of highway that I was supposed to take.

I glanced outside again. The last trace of color in the sky had vanished. Nothing left except thick, heavy black.

The waitress took his order then returned to me and lifted her eyebrows. "You decided on anything, hun?"

"Yeah, I'll have the Special."

She scribbled something on the paper faster than a toddler writing on a wall before you can stop him.

"You got it, hun."

As she walked off, I tried to think about the deal but had a funny feeling I was being watched.

I turned back to the man in the beige coat. Yep, still watching me. Not invasive, just a steady stare.

But why me? There were at least fifteen people, including the guy three tables away smacking like he hadn't eaten in years.

I shrugged, then picked up the mug. No steam. Just bitter, lukewarm black coffee. I sipped it slowly, letting the flavor settle into my mouth. Felt a jolt of energy almost instantly. Something about coffee always did that to me.

The food came shortly after.

By the time my plate was empty, ketchup and all, the rain had arrived. Not a gentle tapping on the window, but a full downpour. Lightning carved through the sky, briefly revealing itself before fading into darkness again.

The waitress returned, holding the carafe.

"Another cup?"

I shook my head and offered a gentle smile. "No thanks. I should probably get going."

She hesitated, her eyes drifting toward the window. "You might wanna wait this storm out. It floods pretty quick around these parts. Every now and then people get stuck out there."

That was the last thing I needed to hear. I knew I should've just gotten gas and left. The burger was good but I could've settled for a bag of chips to hold me over for a while. They even had a couple brands I hadn't seen since I was a kid.

That's what I get for listening to that inner voice and not trusting myself.

"How long you think I should wait?" I asked after finally lifting my head up.

"I'd say a few hours. But it might hold through the night. No way to tell, honestly."

I placed my hand on my forehead. Clearly not her fault, but I felt anger rising as she spoke. I didn't need a weather report—I just needed her approval to leave. To give me the assurance that I could leave and at least be okay.

"I *have* to be in Jordan Heights by morning," I followed up after odd silence.

Her eyes shifted toward the man in flannel. She gave him a quick, wordless cue, and he leaned in from his table.

"Sorry man, but she's right," he said. "Let me see if I can help you. What time tomorrow morning do you need to be there?"

"I have a meeting at eleven but prefer to get

there by nine."

He grinned like a game show host would when they get the answer right. "Well, you're in luck, young man. I know a way that can get you there in less than four hours. You can leave around five when dawn cracks. Storm should be gone or just about."

He seemed confident, but four hours sounded like he was exaggerating. I unlocked my phone, looking at the ETA.

"My GPS says it's six hours. I normally always arrive faster than the GPS… but by two hours sounds like a stretch."

He glanced at my phone then waved his hand downward. "Young man, I know these roads in and out. Been driving for thirty-five years. Trust me. My way is quicker. Your GPS not gonna show it since the entire route isn't paved."

"Is it safe?"

"Safe as a secret," he grinned. "If I can get my big rig through it safely, then I'm sure your Nissan won't be an issue."

I paused for a second, keeping my smile chill.

How does he know what I'm driving?

But I kept it cool, thanking him then turning back to the waitress. "Any hotels close by?"

I prayed that she'd recommend anything but the place across the street. But when her eyes lifted up toward the window, I knew right then I'd just lost that battle with the Lord.

"Anchor Inn. Probably not the luxury you're used to but it's dry and does the trick."

"Guess that'll do," I said with a smile.

The man wrote down the directions for me. After I handled the check, I thanked them, then zipped up and braced myself for the rain. I decided to leave my car at the diner and jog across the street to the inn.

Inside, a blend of mildew and lemon cleaner instantly hit my nose. The clerk barely looked up, and the only expression he gave was a small smile just before sliding me a keycard for Room 4.

The room was simple. Yellowish light filled the front, casting only a small bit near the sink. But this was good enough. I just needed some sleep before finishing my journey.

I dropped my soaked hoodie on the chair and sat down at the edge of the bed.

I thought about Regina. I hadn't checked in with her since I told her I was driving instead of waiting at the airport and risking a canceled flight.

I grabbed my phone and tapped 'Wifey.'

She answered quickly. "Hey."

"Hey," I said, letting my head hit the mattress. "Wanted to let you know that I'm staying in some small town for the night. A bad storm is coming this way."

"Will it affect you making the meeting on time?"

"Not at all," I said, finally showing some excitement. "One of the locals gave me a shortcut that'll take a couple hours off. I'm not missing that meeting for anything."

"Ok," she said, her energy the direct opposite of

mine. "Does it sound safe?"

"Yeah, it *does*… but I'll have my GPS just in case something happens."

"Ok, Micah. Just be safe. Get some rest and text me when you leave in the morning."

It seemed as if she was rushing to get off the phone. Normally, we'd talk for hours when I was away.

"You must be busy," I assumed. I tried to not sound accusatory but I could tell she took it that way.

"I'm just tired, Micah. I was half-sleep when you called."

"At seven?"

My thought came out loud.

"Yes. You must've forgotten I had a long day to-day."

I know she did.

I also knew she missed me.

"Okay," I said. "I'll let you get some rest. Love you."

"Love you too."

She hung up first.

I set my phone on the nightstand and leaned back, staring at the ceiling. It bothered me that she didn't say much, but I knew she just wanted me home.

But what I wanted from her is to know how much these trips meant for the both of us.

As I tried to drift off into sleep, I couldn't help but think about this town. I went from having a weird feeling about this place to now spending the night.

But I closed my eyes and decided to give it to God before I let my mind start wandering again. Maybe this town was just a pit stop—just a strange coincidence.

Or maybe it was somehow part of God's plan.

CHAPTER TWO

5:30 a.m.

I jumped up. The rain was still beating hard against the hotel window. I wasn't supposed to sleep this long. I had to leave now if I had any chance of making it in time.

My bag was still in the car so I threw on yesterday's clothes. Jeans, a collared shirt, and my hoodie that air dried but was about to get soaked again.

I left the key at the counter in the lobby. Didn't bother waiting for the front desk clerk since I paid cash.

Water pooled around my shoes as I crossed the parking lot to the diner where my car sat. Pulling out my keys, I felt something slip from my pocket. I glanced down—it was a folded piece of paper, probably the receipt from last night.

Once I got in, I brushed off and turned the ignition. The engine cranked, and the dashboard illumined before fading.

But there was one light that stayed on.

Low fuel.

"Of course," I muttered.

I was supposed to get gas last night.

And now the place was closed.

I pulled out my phone to search for another station nearby. No signal. I raised it higher. Still nothing. I waited a second but no luck.

I tried sending a quick message to Regina. Just for a check-in and to see if she could track my location and help me find a nearby gas station.

But when I hit send, the screen flashed: *Message Failed.*

Panic started creeping in, but then I remembered the man's directions—written out step by step. There had to be a few stations along the way.

I reached into my pocket for the paper. Empty.

A chill crawled up my spine. *The paper!*

That's what had fallen out when I opened the car door. My only guide… somewhere out there in the rain.

Trying not to panic, I got out and searched for it. But by the time I found it, the ink had smeared. All I could make out was the first direction:

Go forward.

I got back in my car, rubbed my forehead and let out one of the loudest sighs ever.

That paper was my last hope.

"Lord, help me," I cried. And right after, I wondered why I even prayed. God doesn't care that my phone isn't working. Besides, the weather was to blame. And this smeared paper? God isn't gonna make it reappear like He did for stone tablets back in the day. This was real life. Modern times. And I was screwed.

Then a knock on my window.

I looked up. Squinted through the foggy glass.

It was him.

The man from the diner. Same beige coat. Same calm stare.

Should I speed off or run him over?

But something about his calmness grounded me.

Still, I remained cautious. I rolled the window down, only a few inches, just enough to speak.

"Can I help you, sir?"

He gave a slow nod. "I think we can help each other."

I let out a short laugh. "Unless you're headed my way, I don't see how."

He looked around before speaking. "You're going to Jordan Heights, right? Overheard your conversation last night inside the diner. You let me in and I'll make sure we both get there on time."

My eyes narrowed. "But is that where *you're* going?"

The corner of his mouth curved upward. Not really a smile, but enough to let me know something shifted.

"Let's just say our paths happen to run together for a bit."

I locked eyes with him for a moment. Something in me wanted to believe him, but another part of me kept flashing through worst-case scenarios.

"Look," I said, taking the safe route. "How about I give you a couple dollars." I pulled out my wallet, flashed a few bills. "You can catch a cab or do whatever you want with it."

He stepped closer, not looking at the money at all. "There are no cabs out here. And you'll need someone who knows these roads since your Plan A is... ruined."

I caught his gaze drop to the dashboard, to the smeared paper.

Leaning back, I let out a laugh. I'd seen this before. Maybe not in real life, but definitely on television. A man offers a stranger a ride on a quiet road. Some small, backwoods town where no one locks their doors because no one ever expects anything to happen.

Until it does.

I could see it on the news now. Thirty-five-year-old Texas man kidnapped and murdered. Witnesses say they last saw him checking out of a hotel around five a.m. If you have any information, please contact authorities.

And just like the movies, the authorities could be in on it.

Nah, I'm good.

"Listen," I said, holding back more laughter. "How about you just give me the directions and I'll give you the cash. Even if there aren't any cabs around here, you can at least give it to someone else who may be willing to give you a ride. Sorry, I just have this thing with trust."

He locked eyes with me. Not angry, not sad, just focused. And in the midst of it, something changed. Nothing that I would normally feel. I wasn't scared. Maybe I should've been. But I was curious. And in a strange way, I felt that he was right—I did need him.

But I shook it off. Why would I need him? What's wrong with just getting directions from him and continuing this journey alone?

The more I debated, the more the shift got stronger. Something telling me, 'Micah, this is your moment'.

Was I really about to give this guy a ride? Maybe. Last night wasn't a coincidence. And this—it all felt connected with a purpose tied to it.

I glanced at him again. Still patient. I wanted to ask more questions like where he was from, but something inside of me stopped me.

I sighed, hovering over the door lock. "Alright, man… I normally don't do things like this but I guess since I need you as much as you need me, I'll make an exception. But please don't make me regret it."

"You won't," he replied, already moving toward the passenger side. Calm and certain.

Once he got in, he placed his bag between his feet. Didn't say a word at first. Just buckled up and kept his eyes on the road as if he was prepared for the journey of his life.

"Which way?" I asked.

"Go forward." He pointed ahead. "Then a right at the first stop sign."

I gave a slight nod, put the car in drive and pulled

onto the main road.

That word did something to me. It was the only line the storm hadn't erased. There had to be some meaning to it.

Once I made the right at the stop sign, the road narrowed. The space filled with more trees, less gravel and more rocks.

I slowed down a bit to stop the car from bouncing. But only being able to go thirty-five miles per hour, didn't quite meet the short-cut criteria… at least in my opinion.

"So," I said, looking at him. "Is this way quicker than the other guy's way? Or about the same?"

He nodded but kept his eyes straight. "We'll get there in time."

I frowned but bit my tongue. Normally, I'd demand a clearer answer. Especially if my question was direct.

But maybe he was arrogant. Maybe life had worn him down and he just didn't do much talking.

I tightened my grip on the wheel as the rocks rumbled underneath. For a while, that was the only sound in the vehicle.

I reached over and turned on the radio. Static. Tried another station but still nothing. Finally, I cut it off.

After another few minutes, I turned back to the mystery man.

"You know, I don't believe I got your name. Figured we could at least get to know each other. I'm Micah."

"Lior."

I raised my hand slightly expecting him to say something else. Matter of fact, he didn't even say thanks for the ride.

But I figured the more I talk, the more he'd probably open up.

"So, Lior… you from here? That name sounds foreign."

"Hebrew."

My brows lifted. "Oh. Like the book in the Bible? Cool."

Finally, he glanced at me. Letting out the smallest bit of emotion, but it was at least a start.

"Hebrew is more than a book. It's a people. A language. The first ones God called out to follow Him. Abraham was a Hebrew. So was Moses. The language carried their identity… who they were and who they belonged to."

A laugh slipped out before I could stop it. "Thanks for the Bible Study lesson, man. I didn't know all that, honestly."

"Most people don't."

The way he said it made my eyelids crinkle. But like I said, probably just the way he is.

Moments later, I looked down at the dashboard light.

"You know of any gas stations coming up? We're gonna be stuck out here if we don't find one soon."

He looked over at the dashboard. I felt like he challenged my statement in silence.

"Yes," was all he said.

I nodded slightly. At least he felt comfortable that we'd find one soon.

We drove on. Trees continued to line either side of the road. Rain heavy in some parts.

Then the gas needle hit the bottom. I kept looking at it, then back at him, hoping he'd get the memo—or at least say something.

Finally, he spoke. "Turn left at the next intersection."

I squinted, trying to see where he was talking about, but there was nothing.

"You sure?" I asked, half turning toward him.

He just nodded. No words.

I wasn't sold on his confidence but slowed just in case. Good thing I did—at the last possible second, an intersection appeared out of nowhere, and I cut the wheel hard to make the turn.

Almost immediately, it felt different again. Not just the trees and the road, but the rain began to ease. And the night sky was surrendering to the light. The road curved gently, but not to the point where I had to continue to drive slow.

Minutes later—boom, there it was. A gas station. Sitting like a blessing in the middle of nowhere. The kind you anticipate but don't expect.

I parked beside the pump, relief loosening my shoulders.

"You sure you knew this was here?" I teased. "Because honestly, I don't think you did."

"What makes you think that?"

"Well, for one, you didn't say anything as it came

up. It just kinda popped up out of nowhere."

He gave me a studied look. "Did I need to? Seems like you saw it just in time and didn't pass it."

"Would you have let me pass it?"

"No."

"Yeah, right," I mumbled, a grin stretching on my face. Unless he knew I was going to see it, there was no way he would've been able to tell me before I passed it.

I shut the car off, stepped out and reached for my wallet. There was no card reader. I let out a sigh and headed toward the door.

Behind me, the passenger door opened.

"I'll take care of it," Lior said, already getting out.

I paused, waiting for him to catch up. "Are you sure?"

He just smiled, patted me on the back and went inside. A few moments later, he walked out, slipping a receipt into his coat pocket.

"There's a fuel shortage," he said. "I was able to convince them to give us five gallons. But don't worry, we'll pass a few more stations along the way."

I nodded, lifted the nozzle and started pumping. The handle clicked quicker than I expected. Five gallons felt like a drop in a bucket, but I was at least grateful we got something.

We got back in, restarted the engine and eased back on the road. For a while, neither of us said anything. I checked my phone a couple of times, still no service. Maybe the storm knocked out a tower or something.

The radio still didn't work either. After a few more miles of boredom, I glanced over at Lior.

"We're still going the right way, right?"

"Yes."

"Any turns coming up soon? Don't want to be thrown off like last time."

"No."

I chuckled at his clipped calmness but felt the need to address it. "Lior, don't take this personally," I said slowly. "But where I'm from, we take one-word answers as a sign of disrespect."

He turned to me, giving me his full attention. "If I said more, you'd trust me less."

"And what's that supposed to mean?"

"It means sometimes the truth doesn't sound right until you're ready for it."

"What truth?" I said, letting out a frustrated chuckle. "Look, I'm just trying to spark a conversation, but if that's too much then cool. We'll just sit here until you tell me where to turn."

I hated how sharp I sounded, but I was frustrated. He wasn't giving me much to build on.

I took his silence as agreement. It still didn't sit right with me. Luckily, I needed him otherwise he'd be on the side of the road waiting on the next person to give him a ride. It's crazy how rude and ungrateful people can be.

I looked at the clock again. Now 6:45—just over an hour since we'd left town, but it felt longer.

Eventually, my mind drifted to the meeting. I'd been rehearsing it in my head. I'd shake everyone's hand, go over the numbers, then nail the delivery. I already had my pitch. It was polished, precise. I could make them nod without asking too many questions. I knew when to pause, knew when to smile. Knew when to shift my tone just enough to make it feel personal.

The rain eased into a drizzle, a faint mist through the air like dust. The road ahead was slick but not dangerous. Just a thin sheet of water stretching out in a quiet, steady line.

"I'll make it on time," I told myself. I still didn't know how much time I was saving, but figured I'd gained some ground. The mountains were behind us now, fading into the distance like a memory.

About twenty minutes later, we rolled into open country—grassy plains stretching wide, broken only by the occasional fence line. Everything felt flatter and quieter.

A few cars passed, their tires hissing through the wet road, kicking up a light mist as they disappeared ahead. I wondered if any of them were dealing with the same thing that I was—no service, no GPS, just a vague idea of direction and a little bit of hope.

Maybe they were just as unsure as I was. Maybe none of us really knew where we were going. We were all just following pavement, hoping it led somewhere we recognized.

Finally, Lior spoke. "There's another gas station about two miles ahead."

I turned to him, nodding. "So, you really know these roads, huh?"

"Been on them all my life."

"Ahh—so, you from that town I picked you up in?"

"Not *from* there."

I waited on a follow up. Nothing.

"Well, how long have you been there?" I asked, then lifted one hand off the wheel in a small shrug. "But let me know if that's too personal."

He drew in a deep breath then let it out slowly. "Some paths you don't choose. You're just put on them. And after a while, they start to feel like home. Even if they aren't."

I chuckled. "Alright, man. What are you talking about this time? Do you really expect me to know what that means?"

"No."

"So, why say it?"

He stayed silent.

The gas station came into view and he pointed towards it. I slowed down, making the right turn, pulling next to the first unoccupied pump.

"No just means not yet," he finally said. "When the time's right, you'll know everything that you need to know."

He didn't give me a chance to respond. He just opened the car door and stepped out.

He turned toward me just as he was about to shut the door.

"I'll take care of the gas again."

"You sure? I mean, you did get us five gallons earlier."

He raised his hand. "It's the least I will do."

"Cool," I shrugged.

But after he walked away, I thought about what he said. *Least he will do? Not can do?*

What was next?

CHAPTER THREE

Lior had been in the gas station for a while. I couldn't see him through the glass or make out any movement inside.

I shifted in my seat, tapping the steering wheel as my thoughts ran wild. *Was this place getting robbed? Was it Lior? Was he some kind of criminal disguised as an innocent hitchhiker? And if so, would they think I was with him?*

I half-laughed at the thought—but it still lingered in my mind. Truth was, I didn't know him. I didn't know where he was from, what he did for a living or why he happened to be at the diner last night. So, if he was robbing the place, who would believe me? I can see me trying to explain it now: *Officer, I picked this guy up at a diner because he needed a ride. I don't know where I'm at now nor do I know the name of the town I picked him up in, but I'm telling you I had nothing to do with it.*

I wouldn't even believe that if I told it to myself.

Suddenly, I noticed something.

He left his bag inside the car. That old, dusty bag that looked older than he was.

I glanced at the storefront again. No movement.

Curiosity got the best of me. I reached down and carefully picked it up. It was heavier than it looked.

I unzipped it just enough to peek inside. A Bible lay on top, then a small bottle of oil, a glass water bottle and a journal—covered in writing that I'd never seen before.

Without warning, a flash of light caught my eye. For a second, I thought it came from the bag—maybe it did… but when I looked up, Lior was walking out of the store, heading straight for the car.

I zipped it quickly, set it back on the floor and stepped out. I went over to the gas pump, trying to play it cool.

"This place has plenty of fuel," he said, spreading his arms wide and flashing a smile. "You can fill up this time."

I nodded then lifted the nozzle, smirking. "You were in there for a while. For a minute, I thought you might be robbing the place."

I laughed, but he didn't.

He just turned and walked over to the passenger side and got in.

Through the window, I watched him lift the bag and start looking through it. He glanced my way, but I turned before our eyes could meet. I kept my focus on the pump until it stopped.

When I got back in, I asked, "Same way?"

He nodded, eyes still fixed on the bag.

I started the car but checked my phone again before throwing it into gear. Still no bars.

"Man," I muttered. "When's this thing gonna

start working again?"

He looked down at the phone then at me. "You got someone you need to call?"

"Yes, my wife," I said, letting out a dry chuckle. "But come on, man… you don't think not having a working phone is a big deal?"

He shook his head. "I don't own a phone."

"Well, I do." I held mine up, giving it a quick shake. "I do everything on it. Don't you know how many deals I closed on my cell phone?"

He gave a slow nod, like he understood, but didn't approve.

"Sometimes, God disconnects things on purpose. Gives us time to hear Him."

"Oh, yeah, like what?" I said, suspicion rising in my voice. "I hope you're not saying that God purposedly cut my service knowing how bad I need to get to this meeting."

Lior let out a silent sigh. "We'll get there on time."

"And how can you be so sure? You don't know if the rain's gonna get worse… or we could break down, catch a flat… You see how rocky this road is, right?"

He didn't reply right away—just stared out the window like he was watching something that I couldn't see.

Then he finally said, "If you need a guarantee, that means you didn't trust me from the beginning. And if you don't trust me, then why'd you agree to give me a ride in the first place?"

"Because you said we can help each other."

He turned his whole body toward me. "And what part of this journey makes you think we're not?"

This guy had a question for everything.

Luckily, I had a response.

"We've been driving a minute," I said, pointing to the dashboard clock. "And it doesn't even feel like we've made any progress."

"Doesn't feel like or haven't?" he countered.

"Honestly, I don't know."

"And why is that?" he followed up. "Is it because nothing looks familiar to you?"

I let out a slow breath, making it clear I was tired of his endless counters. "It's not about familiarity. It's just… all these roads look the same. Gravel, then asphalt, gas station then repeat. No signs or nothing."

"So, you need signs *and* direction in order to feel safe?"

That question made me pause.

It didn't seem like he was talking about getting to Jordan Heights.

However, this wasn't the time nor place to figure out what he meant. I had to get going.

"Look," I said, finally putting the car in gear. "All I need you to do is guarantee we'll be there by nine or before. Let's cut out the 'get there on time' talk."

He didn't answer.

Instead, he reached across and laid a firm hand on my shoulder.

It wasn't aggressive nor was it all that strong.

But it carried weight. Presence not pressure.

And it grounded me for a moment.

When he pulled his hand back, he leaned back into his seat, shoulders loosening like he'd decided the back and forth was done for now.

The silence that followed felt like a truce—not a full surrender, but enough to clear the air.

I eased onto the road. Lior gave me a couple turns to make, nothing complicated, and before long, we were winding through a stretch of open land again. The sky was still overcast, but brighter now, as if the storm had passed without asking permission.

Minutes later, I let out a long yawn. "I should've asked you to get me some coffee at the last stop," I said. "I barely have any energy."

He turned toward me. "Sounds like you need rest, not a beverage."

The tension was starting to creep in again.

"I'll rest when I close this deal."

"For how long?" he asked. "Until the *next* one?"

I laughed. Didn't really want to waste any more energy on his counters.

As we continued, the road ahead narrowed again. Potholes. Loose gravel. I eased off the gas, letting the car roll through the bumps.

Then out of nowhere, Lior leaned forward and said, "Turn around."

I looked at him sideways. "Wait—what? Why are we turning around?"

He kept his eyes forward. "It's part of the jour-ney."

"Part of the journey? Man, what's the deal with

you?"

Nothing.

But I went ahead and turned around. Nearly got stuck in the mud.

About a hundred feet later, he had me make a quick left.

I rolled my eyes. "See, if my phone was working, we wouldn't have missed that turn."

Lior moved his head upward. "Look in your rear-view."

I glanced up.

In the center of the road was a large hole.

"If we came from the other way," he said. "Your car would've dropped right into it. Sorry for the mud. But sometimes the messier path keeps you from something that'll wreck you."

I didn't say anything. Just kept staring into the rearview, trying to find a flaw in what he said.

But I couldn't.

"Micah," he continued. "I'm not only giving you directions… I'm doing my best to make sure no harm comes your way."

In that moment, I felt humbled.

Maybe Lior wasn't trying to take me the long way just to test my patience. Maybe he was steering me clear of things I couldn't see—things that could stop me from getting to Jordan Heights.

For a while, things got quiet again. I looked over at him to make sure he was still awake. Eyes were wide as ever. Looking ahead. No big movement. Not even a cough.

"So," I said, breaking the quiet. "Where'd you learn to talk the way you do? You've got this way of making everything sound special. Sacred."

He shook his head. "I just speak from the heart."

I let that sit for a minute, watching the lines of the road slip under the hood. "Well, I'd say that's a gift. Anyone in your family talk like that?"

"Yes."

I gave a short chuckle. "Like who—your dad, your mom… or maybe an uncle?"

"My dad."

I nodded. "How about your family? You got a wife? Kids?"

"No."

I chuckled again. I didn't know what was worse—the silence or his answers.

"Alright, Lior," I sighed. "Just let me know if my questions bother you and I'll shut up."

"They don't."

"So, why the one-word answers?"

"Not every man's story fits the questions you ask."

"Yeah, but it's called conversation. Maybe I just expected you to be a little more… I don't know… talkative."

"Ok," he said, turning toward his upper body toward me. "I belong to a different kind of family."

My brows furrowed. "Family is family, right?"

"Yes. But the order is different. Some are born into families the way you're thinking. Others are sent

by their family to do a certain work. And sometimes… those paths cross. They meet in the middle—
maybe to give each other what they're missing."

For a second, I just stared at him, wondering if
we were still talking about family or if he'd switched
to another language mid-sentence.

"Man… you're gonna have to break that down,
cause I'm not following you at all."

He sat there for a moment, as if he was sorting
through his own thoughts. Then he looked at me.

"Micah, let me ask you this… do you know the
difference between being a provider and being a par-
ticipant in your family?"

"Of course I do," I said quickly. "I fall into the
provider category."

"So, I take it you're married?"

"Yep. Married to my beautiful wife, Regina. And
we have two boys… Xavier and Bradley. Ten and
three."

He nodded like he was logging the info.

"Where are you from?"

I thought about it for a second. I'd lived in so
many places. I decided to just give him my whole
background.

"I'm originally from Jacksonville, Florida. Then
moved to Charlotte for about a year. Then Atlanta for
a couple years. Now, I've been in Dallas for the last
three."

"I assume you moved all those places for work?"
I nodded. "Yeah."

"What kind of work do you do?"

My eyes sparkled. This was my type of language. "Sales. I'm the lead Sales Executive for my company. Been there twelve wonderful years. Climbed the corporate ladder, you know."

I wasn't trying to brag, but I wasn't scared to let people know how God has blessed me and my family. Too many folks scared to talk about their careers.

Lior didn't react much. No nod, no smile, just his usual posture.

"You go to church?"

His tone didn't come off like a casual question, it felt more like a test. Not really judgmental, but something that required more than a yes or no.

"Of course," I said. "Gotta keep God first in my life."

We passed a car that seemed to slow down as it drove by. Lior kept his eyes on them until they disappeared around the curb.

"You spend a lot of time with your family?" he asked.

I gave him a thumbs up. "Yep. We take vacations every summer. Went to Florida last year. Cruise coming up later this year."

"My question was about time, not trips."

I sat up a little straighter and gave him a look. His words landed harder than I expected. Still, I didn't want to come off rude with my reply.

"Yes, I spend time with my family. I see them every day—well, except for the few trips like this one."

He registered my reply with a nod. "Does your

wife work?"

"Nope. She stays home. Takes care of the boys."

"Do you think that fulfills her?"

"Yeah, I think so. She complains every now and then about being bored, but at least she gets to rest. Shop when she wants. Sleep in most mornings. Catch up with her friends... If I were her, I'd love that life."

Lior went silent again. It felt like he was deciding between responding to what I already said... or asking more questions.

He chose the latter.

"How would you rate your communication with her?"

"Ten out of ten," I bragged. "She tells me how she feels and I do the same."

As soon as the words left my mouth, something about them didn't sit right. Not that they weren't true... but they didn't tell the whole story either.

Regina and I haven't been on the same page lately.

But that wasn't any of Lior's business.

Besides, our communication was still there—it's just we needed to tweak it a bit. Spend more time together... take more tips. Regina loved the beach.

I happened to glance at the time and my focus shifted abruptly.

"Listen, Lior. I know we talked about this but I just want to do another time check. We still good?"

Lior looked up at the sky, back to the road, and never the clock. "Yes. We'll get there at the right time. Not a minute early, not a second late." He let the words breathe before adding, "You're focused on the clock, I'm focused on the arrival."

I let out a short laugh, part amused and part disbelief.

"Look man, that sounds deep, but I'm trying to get there so I can shower and prepare myself. I don't want to get there late and have to rush."

Lior let out a sigh, the kind that said more than words.

But who cares what he thought? So what if he was tired of me asking about the time? I was tired of him not giving me a straight answer.

Hopefully my service starts working soon so I won't need him. I didn't want to kick him out, but I'd definitely stop somewhere and tell him he'd have to find a way on his own.

I shifted my thoughts. My mind was on the commission check I'd get. Maybe I'd finish the patio. We'd talked about it ever since we bought the house. Regina wanted a spot to sit outside, book in hand, sipping tea—or maybe a little wine in the evenings.

Or maybe just take a trip to South Padre. That's the one place Regina kept saying she wanted to go. Yeah… that's exactly what we needed. Time together. Away from the norm.

I kept driving, picturing the sand and the water. Maybe the beach wouldn't fix everything, but we could at least enjoy ourselves.

"Seems like you're in deep thought," Lior's voice broke through the silence. "Mind sharing what's on your mind?"

I titled my head, snapping out of my thoughts. "Nope, not at all. I was just planning our next trip. Regina wants to go to a particular beach."

He inspected his fingernails, no sense of urgency in his response.

"What about you? You love the beach?"

I shrugged. "I mean, it's ok. Honestly, I'm more of a city guy when it comes to vacations."

He nodded, as if filing that away, then said, "Sounds like y'all have a lot of compromises and sacrifices. Would you agree?"

"Nope. We may not agree on everything but we know how to meet in the middle."

"And would you say that's done in silence or communication?"

"Communication," I answered, then cleared my throat—partly to steer the focus on him.

Truth was, his questions were starting to poke at things I hadn't thought about in a long time. Maybe they were waking something up, though I couldn't tell yet if I liked where it was headed. So, I changed the subject.

"What about you? You love traveling?"

"I do. But not the beach. I see water all the time. I prefer rides like this."

I let out a chuckle. "Really? So, your idea of a vacation is going on journeys with strangers?"

He inclined his head. "Everyone's a stranger until you get to know them."

I faked a smile.

Not because I wanted to frown or anything, but

because his punchlines seemed to hit at the right time. So, right that I felt the need to call him out.

I switched hands on the wheel then turned to him. "Lior, it really sounds like you rehearsed some of these lines. They're too good."

His eyes lit up. "You mean like prepared for times like this?"

"That's exactly what I mean," I said, pointing to his smirk. "It's like you ask questions that you already know the answer to."

His smirk didn't fade.

"Maybe I do," he said, leaning back. "Or maybe I just ask questions that you've already been answering—just not out loud."

I went quiet, replaying our conversations in my head. What questions had I been answering without realizing it? I'd mentioned my family, my job... even my travel habits. But was I missing something? Or was he just trying to piece me together from the little things I shared?

"I like to help people," he continued. "Not just to their destination but show them the way."

The way he said it made me wonder if he meant more than the road we were on. Like he was steering toward something deeper than just a drive to Jordan Heights.

"We *are* still talking about physical destination, right? Or is this just another one of your metaphors?"

He let out a breath and paused before speaking. "Micah, one thing I've learned along the way is that most people think joy comes from carving out a life that they designed. But life really starts when you submit to the one who already carved it out for you."

At first, I thought he was just talking in general… but something in his tone made me wonder if this was aimed at me.

I leaned back and let my hand rest on the wheel. "So, where are you going with this?"

He hesitated before responding. "Micah, I see a lot of good in you. You're a hard worker and I'm sure a great husband and father. But I also think you may be working hard for the wrong things."

My breath eased out, quiet but heavy. "Nah, I work hard for my family. To provide for them and give them the life I never had."

"And what exactly might that be?"

"A steady home and enough money to keep it that way. I don't want my kids packing up every few months like I did growing up."

He rested his hand on his chin. "How old were you the first time you remember moving?"

I shrugged. "I don't know… probably like six."

He nodded. "You said you moved your family a lot too, right? Do you think you moved them more times than your parents moved you?"

My grip tightened on the wheel. I saw where this was going.

"It's probably about the same," I replied. "But I move them because of promotions not evictions."

Lior gave a faint nod, holding his head upward. "So, in other words, your parents moved because they had to. And you moved…simply because you wanted to."

"And something's wrong with that?" I barked. "I wanted to provide for my family and I did."

"But whose life really gets better when you move? There's or yours?"

I tapped the wheel and shook my head. Lior obviously didn't know what it was like to be in the corporate world. Probably never had a job of any value in his life.

"I make sure every move is something that we all want," I said. "I carefully plan neighborhoods, school districts, demographics—everything."

Lior leaned back, keeping his eyes on me. "But why so many moves? From the way you talk, it's not about the address—it's like you're chasing something you can't quite name. Listen, every house is built by someone, but the One worth finding is the one God builds. If you're not rooted there, you'll keep moving, looking for what you already have."

I let out quick laugh. "Listen, man. I have tripled my salary since I first started with this company. And my moves are different than when I was growing up. Imagine coming home from school telling your kids I got a promotion and moving to a new city versus telling them that we're getting evicted and have to move out soon."

Lior tilted his head. "I see where you're going with that. One gives you barely enough time to pack boxes while the other gives you a little more time to prepare hearts. Maybe even do a little convincing. But either way, it still takes them from what they know."

I let out another sigh but kept my eyes on the road, not wanting to give him the satisfaction of a response. Everyone can make assumptions—but it doesn't mean they're right.

The sound of the road filled the silence, and for a few miles, neither of us said anything. I thought about all the places we'd called home and how each one came with its own trade-offs. Overall, I think I did a great job.

Lior broke the silence.

"What does Regina think about Dallas?"

I still wasn't ready to talk to him but figured it would make the time go by at least.

"She loves it. She loves the church, the newness of the area—a lot of things."

"She ever mentions what she might not like about it?"

"There's nothing to dislike about it," I said, shaking my head. "Especially for her. She has everything she needs—well, except her family but she doesn't really miss them."

"And how do you know that?"

"Because she only says something after we go down to visit. It's like the trip reminds her they exist, and then she'd be fine again once we're back home."

I expected a response, but Lior just let the moment breathe.

A minute or two later, he rubbed his hands together as if his inventory taking was complete.

"So, from what I can gather, it sounds like you work, provide *financially*, while your wife takes care of the household."

I let out a short, disbelieving laugh. He really thought that was all I did? I fixed things. Built things. Me and a couple guys had even put together a swing set for the boys. Who does he think he is, trying to piece me together?

"Lior, I'm not just some guy who makes money and call myself a provider. I care about way more than just money."

He nodded slowly, looking out the window before saying anything.

"I'm sure you do, Micah. But money sounds like it's at the top of your list. Needing validation is a close second. God's somewhere in there too and then your family."

I chuckled. "And how do you even know this?"

He hesitated, rubbing his beard like he was pulling words out from somewhere deep.

"I've watched a lot of good men mistake movement for growth. Currency for connection. Promotions for provision. Their minds drift far from where they should be. They think it's okay to miss a game for a business trip. To ignore their wife's ideas because it doesn't align with their own needs."

I let out another chuckle, sharper this time, with a sigh buried underneath. "Lior, everything I do is for my wife. That house we bought—that was for her. She got the car she kept talking about. Trips when she wanted them. I've made sure she's good."

He turned his head slightly, eyes narrowing just

enough to let me know he was about to poke at something.

"And besides what *you* give her, what does she like to do on her own?"

The question caught me off guard. My grip loosened on the wheel as I searched for something—anything—that came to mind. The past six months flashed through my head.

"Honestly, man, she doesn't do much. She'll throw a random idea out here and there, but never really follow through on it. But besides that, she just sits home, phone in one hand while the remote in the other. I hate to say it, but it's like she's lost her drive for life."

He leaned back and let my words breathe before speaking again. "Do you think you pushed her drive away with all these moves?"

My first instinct was to say no, but the question did stick with me. Maybe I did. Or maybe she didn't have a drive to begin with.

"I don't think so," I said. "If I did, I'm sure she would've said something."

"Maybe she did," he said quietly. "And silently sacrificed her desires for yours."

I smirked, trying to shrug it off. "Nah… Regina's not the type to just keep quiet if something's bothering her."

"That's what you think," he said, turning his gaze out the window. "Sometimes people stay silent to keep the peace. And that silence isn't weakness, it's exhaustion."

The words slipped past my defense, settling in my chest. I replayed conversations in my head. The ones when Regina was excited about moving. But I'd be lying if I said I didn't remember the times she cried as she hugged her friends goodbye. How they'd slowly fade out her life until she had no one besides me and the boys.

"I don't know where this went wrong," I admitted. "All I wanted was the best for them."

Lior's voice softened, but the weight didn't. "I know you did, Micah. But remember, what *you* think is best, is not always gonna be what *she* thinks is."

"Ok… how do I fix this?" I asked. "I want to see her smile again."

Lior drew in a deep breath and let it out slowly. "If you really want to fix your life, you've got to figure out where it started to fall apart. Until you find the root, you're just trimming the weeds."

CHAPTER FOUR

The waiter tucked the menus under his arm as he walked away. I leaned back in my seat, letting my eyes scan the room. This place was nice. Brick walls, low lights, real candles on every table. Jazz playing from the hidden speakers.

I was proud of myself for picking this restaurant. From the outside, it looked like any other place in Atlanta. But inside? A different story. Warm. Intentional. Grown. The perfect place for me and my bride to spend an evening together.

Most of the tables were full, couples leaned in close, some talking low, others just eating and smiling between bites. No one checking their phones. No one looking like they're ready to leave. It was the kind of place people came to enjoy being where they were.

Then I looked across the table at Regina. She hadn't said much since the waiter left. She just twirled her straw, letting the ice clink quietly like she was keeping a rhythm. Her lips had that soft gloss she wears when she wants the night to mean something.

That burgundy dress fit her just right.

And sitting there, it hit me—I couldn't remember the last time I really looked at her like this.

She laced her fingers together and rested her elbows on the table. "So… what made you bring me somewhere this nice tonight?"

My chest tightened. The pressure rose. That quiet pressure knowing I was about to lie—or at least not tell the full truth.

I sat up straighter, adjusted my napkin even though it didn't need adjusting. She kept her eyes on me and it made me feel cornered. So, I said the first thing that came to mind.

"I just wanted us to go out."

She flashed her sexy smile. "Aww, thank you, Micah. You got it right this time."

She meant that.

And that made me feel even worse.

I should've just told her the real reason from the jump. Gotten it out the way. Not have her think this fancy, Buckhead restaurant was just because.

I needed to reroute my anxiety somewhere else. Somewhere that didn't keep me under the microscope. "How's your drink?" I asked, shifting again.

She took a quick sip. "It's actually pretty good, but why haven't you touched yours?"

I blushed. Truthfully, I was too nervous to drink. But I also didn't want to just sit there and make it seem like something was wrong. So, I picked up the glass and brought it to my lips, taking just enough to taste.

"Yeah, this is good. Very smooth."

Setting it back down, I rested my arms on the table. The tension sat deep and I kept running through how I should tell her, but nothing felt right except to just come out and say it.

"I got the promotion."

She studied me for a second, as if she was making sure she heard me right. Once I forced a smile, her eyes lit up.

"Really, Micah? The Lead Sales Exec position?"

I nodded.

"That's so amazing! How come you waited until now to tell me?"

"I wanted to surprise you." The words came out fast, before I could think them through.

She reached across the table and kissed me on the lips. Still smiling, still holding onto the moment.

But I couldn't match her expression. And she noticed.

Her smile faded. "What's wrong, Micah?"

I hesitated, then drew in a deep breath, preparing myself to let it out. "If I accept the promotion, we have to be in Dallas by July."

"Dallas?" Her head tilted slightly, a frown settling in. "Wait… are you saying we'd have to move there?"

I nodded, then my eyes dropped to the table. "Yeah. The company is centralizing leadership in the South region, and Dallas will be the new hub."

She leaned back, crossing her arms. That unusual excitement she just showed was now long gone.

"So, this is what this dinner is about," she said, tone sharp. "Here I am thinking we were just enjoying a date night for once. I should've known this was just another one of your… *presentations*."

I didn't have anything to say. She was right. Regina and I only went out when it was to celebrate something. And besides our birthdays and anniversary, the only thing we'd been celebrating were my accomplishments at work.

I reached for her hand. "Honey, I told them I'd talk it over with you first. But listen, I *do* need to make a decision by Monday."

She pulled her hand away quickly.

"Monday, Micah? It's Saturday. Why would you tell them you'd decide that quick?"

"Because it's a big opportunity for me—well for us. You've been complaining about this Atlanta traffic for a long time. Dallas is different. You know that. Remember when we visited my cousin out there a few years back and you said you loved it?"

"Just because I loved it doesn't mean I want to move there."

I blinked, trying not to roll my eyes. "But why not?" I challenged. "You want to just complain about traffic all day or live somewhere more spread out? Newer?"

Her lips moved a little, like she wanted to deny it, but couldn't. I just took the opportunity to further convince her.

"With this new salary, we can finally get a house. Look at how long we've been praying for one."

I took out my phone and showed her a couple houses that I'd saved on Zillow. "See, this one has a movie room, game room, office and four bedrooms. Even got an extended patio."

That grabbed her attention for a second. But after flipping through the photos, she shook her head.

"But Micah what about our family? We're already far enough from them now."

"I've thought about all that. We can just fly instead of drive, and honestly, we'll probably see them more from there than we do now."

She drew in a deep breath and stared at the table. "Micah, I need time to think. Not just a couple of days. You really should've said something about this before. Did you not know this job would be in Dallas before you applied?"

I turned my head to the side, looking at the waiter as he walked by. Hoping that by watching him carry a customer's plate, it would give me time to think.

Truthfully, yes—I'd known the job was in Dallas. And that was one of the main reasons I applied. I loved Atlanta but I just wasn't making any money here.

"I know it's tough," I said after a second. "But the window is tight. It's now or never. There's no telling when another opportunity like this will come up."

She didn't say anything. Just looked at me like she was holding back a thousand thoughts.

But slowly, her expression softened. Her tension eased. And it was as if something was changing inside of her. Maybe I'd said the right things? Maybe she was really considering it?

On the flip side, I knew this wasn't easy for her. She'd finally started finding her rhythm here. New friends, new hangouts. But none of it was giving us the financial freedom that we needed. None of it was investing or paying off our debt. The promotion was almost double my salary. And that's just the base salary. Commissions and extra bonuses would put it well over.

I'd been praying for a breakthrough every night. This had to be God's answer... right? You pray for provision, and suddenly the door cracks open with a promotion and covers relocation? That's not a coincidence—that's favor. I'd been tithing, staying consistent, cutting back on stuff I used to do. No, I wasn't perfect but I was making progress. And now I was walking through a door that finally opened for me.

The waiter came over, balancing two ceramic plates. He placed them down gently, offering a warm smile.

"Here's the roasted duck for you," he said, sliding it in front of me. "And the sea bass for you," he said to Regina. "Can I get you two anything else?"

I looked at Regina but she was already shaking her head.

"No, I think we're good."

"Enjoy," he replied, then hurried away.

We both reached for our forks. For a while, neither of us spoke. The food was excellent, but the silence was louder than the flavor.

I glanced at her. She was chewing slowly, looking

down at her plate.

"You like it?" I asked.

She looked up, gave me a quick observation before speaking.

"It's good," she said, voice soft.

I smiled. "Yeah. They weren't playing."

That's all we said for a moment, but even those few words felt like a step forward. Maybe she was starting to see how this could be better for us.

Still, the quiet stretched. And by the time I was almost done with my meal, the question was pressing against my chest. I needed to know where she stood—was she actually considering it or just looking for a way to say no?

"How are you feeling?" I asked. "Normally, you'd be excited about relocations and promotions. What's changed?"

After a second or two, she looked up. Not directly at me, but it was good enough.

I held my breath, watching her face for any shift or sign of hope.

And then, there it was.

She exhaled, slow and heavy, like the words had been pressing against her ribs.

"Ok," she said quietly. "I don't really agree with this move—but I'm sure you prayed about it and God said it was the right move. If so, I don't want to go against *Him*."

I gave a partial smile. Truthfully, I hadn't *really* prayed about it.

Not the way Regina meant. Not with surrender.

Not with being okay if He said no. It was more like, 'God please allow Regina to be ok with this move because I am.'

But I had to give her a response that showed confidence.

"Of course, I prayed. I really believe this is something that God wants us to do."

A little conviction crept in as I spoke, but I pushed it down. Everything was moving so fast, and I'd already put too much into this to start showing doubt now. I just needed her to see it the way I did.

The waiter showed up right on cue, asking if we needed anything. Regina sat up straighter and folded her napkin in half like she was snapping out of a thought.

"We'll take a dessert menu," I said before she could say no.

She gave me a smile. I smiled back. In my eyes, the night was good.

"Remember you said you wanted one of those ham hock things in the back?"

She shook her head, chuckling. "It's a *hammock.* And yes, that would be nice."

"Cool. I'll make sure I get one of those."

I pulled out my phone and opened up the offer sheet, hoping that would get her to smile a little more.

"If I accept, they'll want to fly us out in a couple of weeks. We can check out some neighborhoods to make sure we find something that's good for the three of us."

She hesitated, glancing down for a second before

meeting my eyes again. There was a quiet shift in her expression.

"For the four of us," she said, touching her stomach.

A rush went through my chest. "Wait, are you serious? Why am I just now finding out?"

She raised her head. "I took a test this morning, but nothing's confirmed with my doctor yet. I was going to tell you earlier but when you said you wanted to take me out tonight, I figured I'd wait."

This felt like a blessing in the making. A new baby could keep Regina's days full, give her a reason to not resent the move.

I kept my tone steady. "This won't change anything about the move," I said. "I'll make sure you get a good doctor. And we can fly your mom out if we need to so she can help with everything."

She looked at me, her mouth parting like she wanted to say something, but decided not to. She just drew in a deep breath, opening her mouth to let out a breath. I could picture it all playing out in her head—the logistics, the timing, the stress.

"Trust me, honey," I said. "It'll all work out."

The waiter returned, ready to take our dessert order.

"Let's do the peach cobbler," I said, handing the menu back then looked at Regina. It was her favorite.

She didn't object. I even joked about how she always said she didn't want dessert, then ate half of it anyway. That got a small smile out of her.

The cobbler came out warm and sweet, and we

dug in. She only had a couple bites so I ate the rest.

Once we paid the bill, we headed to the car. I opened the door for her like always, and she slid in without saying much. I got in, letting the windows down slightly, breathing in the cool air.

"You good?" I asked as I buckled in.

"Yeah," she said. "Just full... and tired."

I reached over and touched her belly, letting my hand rest there for a second.

"We're really doing this, honey. New chapter, bigger family. I think this gonna be a great move. I can feel it."

I turned on some music. Something chill and familiar. I then started talking about more real estate listings. I told her how we could paint the kitchen whatever color she wanted. How we could finally get that open layout she'd been pinning pictures of. How the backyard could be big enough for a swing set, a grill, even a little blow-up pool for Xavier and our unborn child.

I felt hopeful. Like I was finally ahead. Finally catching my breath after years of grinding just to stay afloat. This was more than a promotion—it was a reset. A chance to leave behind the noise, the stress, the cycle. A chance to breathe.

A chance to give her more. More of me. More peace. More life.

CHAPTER FIVE

"Sounds like you had your mind made up long before you even mentioned the move to your wife," Lior said after giving me directions to turn on a road.

"I did," I said, looking toward him. "Something wrong with that? I think it's okay to want to feel confident about it myself before bringing it to her."

"That depends on if you truly value her opinion or just want to hear her say yes."

"Actually, both," I said, laying it straight. "I think every man wants their wife to understand how the umbrella works, you know."

Lior tilted his head. "Umbrella—like the one Paul talks about in Corinthians?"

I crinkled my eyes, trying to remember if that was the correct reference. I believed it was, but I wasn't about to let him hear any doubt in my voice.

"Exactly," I said, lifting my hand in an exaggerated arch, almost touching the roof of the car. "At the top is God, then Jesus, then me... and finally, Regina."

He nodded. "So, you're fully submitted to God?"

"I am."

He didn't blink, just moved on to the next question.

"Has things changed for the better since the move to Dallas?"

"Of course, it has," I said, grinning. "My commute is much better, my colleagues are better—well, there are a couple I could live without… but overall, I'd say it was the right move."

"I was talking about better between you and your wife."

Oh. I cleared my throat. "Umm, yeah… I mean, things are kinda a mess with our toddler, me working a little more than I expected… but I think we're good."

Lior didn't give a response. But it didn't matter—I felt his judgment without him even saying anything. Yeah, things weren't as good as we thought they were going to be, but is anything ever? Besides, there were a lot of good things to look at—we lived in a great neighborhood with one of the best school districts in the state.

But even with those high notes, Lior's question made me think a little deeper.

Are you submitted to God?

I replayed my answer. It sounded right. But why does it feel like he can see something I can't?

I snapped out of it when I saw the time. "Ok, man, we still on track?"

"We're fine."

I shook my head, time was ticking. "Nah, I need

more than that, Lior. What time are we getting there? There's no way I can drive this slow on this bumpy road and make it on time."

"Fast can't carry what faith is meant to build."

"And slow can't carry me to this meeting on time."

Lior's tone didn't rise but it landed heavy. "Then I guess you'll have to decide what matters more—arriving when you want or arriving on time."

I dismissed him with a wave. I wasn't trying to be disrespectful but tired of hearing his nonsense.

And to be honest, I was starting to believe he wasn't who he thinks he is. Was he really a wise man or just a crafty guy who knew how to stall. Didn't really have the answers but could make you believe that he did.

The road dipped suddenly, and the tires kicked up a splash of mud that slapped the side of my car. Wasn't bad, but enough to grab my attention.

Then, a deer just standing in the middle of a field, stared at us like we didn't belong out here. Maybe we didn't. This wasn't my route. None of this was. All I wanted to do was get to Jordan Heights. On time.

I should've just handed Lior the money and had him write down directions. Or I could've figured it out myself.

I felt bad for feeling that way, but everything that came out of his mouth sounded like judgment. Not once did he say, 'That was a good move,' or, 'I'm proud of you for stepping up.' Nothing. Just questions and metaphors as if I was a bad husband and father.

Yeah, I missed a game or two. Maybe didn't take Regina out as much as I should've. But I never let them feel unloved. Besides, Regina went to all of Xavier's games. That's the whole point of partnership. The kids had one parent holding the house down and the other out making the money that paid for the house. That *was* balance. It wasn't perfect, but what family is?

I glanced at Lior again, and the thought settled in deeper. This man was not who I thought he was. All that talk about timing and trust, but really, he didn't have a plan. No map. No GPS. Not even a decent estimated time of arrival.

I'd had enough.

I started plotting. I was gonna let him out at the next gas station. I'd give him a few dollars, wish him well, and ask someone else for directions. Somebody normal. Somebody with a phone that worked, or at least a voice that didn't sound like it came from a mountain cave.

I should've listened to my dad. He always told me to be careful if I ever picked up a stranger. He said it every time we passed a hitchhiker growing up. "I don't care if they're limping or crying—if they look suspicious, don't you let them in your car."

He told me this story about his cousin, Jerome, who gave some lady a ride back in the '80s. Said she was sweet, good looking, but when he dropped her off and looked back—nobody was there. Door still locked. Seat belt untouched. I was too young to know if he was serious, but he never laughed when he told it.

And then there was that story I saw on the news last year. A family in Oklahoma picked up a man walking down the side of the highway. Turned out he'd escaped from a prison. Thank God they survived and the police caught the guy. But that could've gone far left.

Lior didn't *look* dangerous, but I'm sure the man in Oklahoma didn't either. Neither did that lady in my dad's *story*.

"Deep thought again?" he said.

I didn't even want to look at him so I kept my eyes on the road. "Any gas stations coming up? I'm getting a little hungry."

"There's one at the end of this dirt road. We'll ride through a small town—like the one I met you at."

I hesitated but then blurted out. "Is it cool if I drop you off there?"

The second it left my mouth, I wanted to slap myself on the forehead. *Why did I ask him that out loud?* I should've just made up an excuse when we got there. Or better yet, send him in the store and speed off. That way I wouldn't have to explain anything.

But the goodness in me wouldn't let me do that.

He chuckled. "Why do you want to drop me off? I plan on being with you the entire way. But if you want to continue this journey on your own, then I understand."

I squinted at him, barely hiding the skepticism rising in my face. He'd said from the start that he was headed my way, but let's be real—how much of a co-incidence is that? Jordan Heights isn't New York City. You don't just *happen* to be going to a small town at the same time.

I shifted in my seat, fingers tightening on the wheel. "Tell me this, Lior—how does a stranger just happen to be sitting in the one diner I pull into, staring at me like he's been waiting on me… then shows up again at dawn saying he's headed to the same town I am? How is any of this random?"

He looked at me, unbothered. "Because it's not," he said. "We serve a God who orders steps. Maybe you thought you stopped at that diner because you were tired or needed gas. But maybe the real reason was bigger than that. Maybe it was so our paths would cross."

How does he even know I was tired? I caught myself shaking my head. *He probably just saw how I downed the coffee and put two and two together.*

"Alright," I said, glancing at him. "Tell me… where were you before we met?"

He looked out the window before answering. "Same place as you."

I frowned. "Okay, but how did you get there? Did someone drop you off and you were just waiting on the next person to come along?"

His gaze returned to me, steady. "I received a command, and I obeyed."

I covered my mouth to keep from laughing. *Something was mentally wrong with this guy.* I should've searched that bag a little longer—maybe he had some of that liquid courage hiding in there. Or something worse. Whatever he was on, I didn't think it was doing him any favors.

I let the laugh fade before speaking. "So, what about me stood out? Did you hear that inner voice saying, 'hey, this is the guy'?"

"Yes," he said, simply. "It's the same voice that led you to stop when you had no reason to."

My eyes widened for a second, but I shook it off. I had said those same words when I pulled up to the diner.

Nah, this was just a coincidence.

At least I think it was.

"If you can really hear this voice and your job is to ride with me... for whatever reason, then I need another sign to believe you. How about you close your eyes and tell me the landmarks that's coming up. But not until my signal."

Lior closed his eyes, head lowered slightly, like he was tuning into something.

Once we got by the sign ahead, I gave my command. "Alright, go."

With his head still lowered, Lior spoke quickly as if he could still see. "Welcome to Cedar Bluff. Now a church with a rusted bell. Right here, that's a farm with a big house behind it. Upstairs light is the only light on."

I chuckled, still not fully believing him. "Man, anybody can do that. I could call out most of the things I see on my way to work."

He still had his eyes closed and head lowered.

"What about the two deer standing by the fence line? Or the white pickup parked about a hundred yards from them? You think those are just memory too?"

Finally, he lifted his head. Everything we passed was exactly as he said.

A weight pressed into my chest. My breath stalled for a moment, like the air itself had thickened. *How did he know all this?*

"Alright," I finally said. "I get that this could be God. But what about me makes me the perfect candidate for this journey?"

Lior's lips curved into a smile. "That's the part you'll find out soon."

"Why not now?"

He shook his head, his tone carrying both patience and warning. "It's not the time. And consider yourself blessed for even getting that much proof. Remember what's written: 'Do not put the Lord your God to the test.'"

Suddenly, I felt something slow me down. Calm, yet powerful. I couldn't even speak for a few minutes.

"Turn up here," Lior said.

I turned, and just like that, a town appeared. Similar to the last ones. A boarded-up post office, a few tiny houses, and just ahead, a gas station.

"Pull into this store," he said.

As I pulled in, Lior unbuckled his seatbelt and got out quickly. "I'll go in."

"But I need to use the restroom."

"It's around back."

I followed his gaze. "Ok. Can you grab me something to snack on?"

He gave me a quick nod then stepped out.

I got out, used the restroom then came back to the car and waited. Tried my phone again. Nothing. I couldn't recall any time I'd gone this long without being able to use my phone.

A few minutes later, Lior stepped out of the store holding a small plastic bag. Once he got in the car, he pulled out a bottle and handed it to me.

"Here you go."

I looked down at it. "Wait. I said I was hungry. Why are you giving me milk?"

"This is better for you right now," he said, pulling a sandwich out for himself.

"And what makes you think that?"

"This milk is all you can handle for right now."

I turned towards him, ready to snatch the sandwich out of his hand. "Man, what I look like? An infant or something?"

He let out a short laugh. "No, you don't *look* like an infant… But let's just say this will keep you sharp and clear for now. Once you're ready, we can stop again and get you some solid food."

He took a bite, keeping his eyes forward.

I sat back, still holding the bottle, heat rising in my chest. I wanted to tell him to get out. He could have the milk and the sandwich for all I care.

But lowkey, I needed him. At least for a little while longer. Until my phone started working.

I twisted off the cap and took a sip. Vanilla. It

was cold and chalky, thicker than I expected, and it lingered in my mouth longer than I liked. It wasn't terrible, just underwhelming.

I pulled out of the parking lot and he guided me back in the same direction we'd just left, as if he'd made me come this way just for some milk.

The small town disappeared behind us in seconds. The road stretched ahead again, cracked and uneven but at least familiar. I took another sip, half out of frustration, half because it was all I had.

Then I thought about Regina. She was probably worried sick.

"You're always this anxious?" Lior blurted out.

I cleared my throat, trying to act like I didn't just spend the last couple minutes spiraling. "What do you mean?"

"You keep checking your phone, asking how long before we get there… It's like you don't rest. Or trust anyone."

I let out a chuckle. "No offense, but yeah, not having control of my situations scares me. I have a family to get home to."

"And you will."

He turned towards the window, his eyes scanning the scenery.

"What time does your wife normally wake up?" he asked.

The question threw me off. I looked at him, but he just kept his head turned, watching the trees like it was a casual question.

"Probably ten or eleven. She sleeps in on Thursdays. Xavier rides to school with our nanny."

"So, she's not up yet," he mused.

"I think she is. Especially knowing I'm out of town."

Lior drew in a breath, then went on to his next question. "You have any close friends?"

I nodded. "Yeah, I got a few. Mostly people from my church, though. Older guys but they're pretty solid. Huge change from the people I grew up with."

"What makes them so different?"

I exhaled through my nose. "Most of the guys I grew up with are still doing what we did as kids, man. No growth. No money mindset or anything. Just running the streets chasing you know what."

"Do you miss them?"

"Sometimes. But every time I'm around them, it reminds me why I left in the first place."

He nodded. "What about your wife? Does she still hang around old friends or is it similar to your situation?"

"Yeah, it's about the same. But she's big on getting together with couples from the church. Sometimes that's cool but sometimes they can be a little extra."

"Explain."

I lifted a shoulder. "Honestly, they seem fake sometimes. Always happy. Smiling nonstop. Like they don't have problems."

"Do you smile when you're with them?"

I rubbed the back of my neck. "Most of the time.

But that's only so I don't look like the grumpy husband. It's easier to just match their energy."

"Would you say grumpy is how you feel inside, just don't want to show it?"

I spotted a small animal run across the road and kept my eyes on it until it ran into the woods. That gave me time to think about his question. Grumpy may not have been the correct word, but there was always a shift in my mood when I got around them.

"Listen," I said. "I just don't see how people can be happy all the time. Life is hard. I don't want to sit here and pretend like I have it all together. But whenever they're around, it seems like pretending is all I do."

"How would you rate your relationship with your wife on a scale from one to ten?"

Lior's questions were coming steady like a stressful interview, not giving me much time to think.

I slowed down, not wanting to reveal a number. "Overall, I'd say we're good, but I can't lie… Regina complains and compares me to the other men in our small group at church. Not really in a bad way, but she's quick to point out what so and so did for their wife. She fails to realize that doing things are a two-way street. There's plenty of things I can point out about her."

Lior nodded but didn't speak. I honestly felt bad for speaking negative about Regina. Up until that point, most of everything I'd said about her had been positive. But Lior seemed to know how to pull the truth out of me.

After a minute or two, he spoke. "Micah, some people smile through pain because they know God still has them. It's not easy, but when you know there's a higher power looking after us, it gives us a reason to be grateful."

I nodded slowly, but something in my chest tightened. I wasn't sure if what I felt was conviction... or just frustration. Maybe both.

Lior glanced over again. "Was there ever a time you felt like your house was full of joy yet you didn't feel it?"

I let out a quiet breath, eyes fixed on the road. And then it hit me. "Yeah," I said, my voice low. "There was this one evening…"

CHAPTER SIX

My phone rang just as I pulled into the driveway. It was John, my manager.

I sighed, leaning back against the headrest. All I wanted was to go inside, kick off my shoes, eat whatever Regina cooked, then pass out on the couch. But I answered anyway, as politely as my mood would allow.

"Hey, John. Sup?"

"Hey, Micah," he said with a burst of energy like he didn't just work the same shift I did. "Just got off the phone with Harper's broker. We have the lowest rates on the table, but they don't believe it's good enough to seal the deal. Think you can take a look at the exhibits tonight and see what else we can do?"

I let out a silent sigh. I'd been working on this deal all week, and it was the last thing I wanted to see.

Still. I knew what was at stake.

"Yeah, I'll take a look," I said. "But just so you know, we are pretty close to the margin floor with this one."

"I know," he sighed. "See if we can cut it two or

three points. They're similar to that Mitchell case you worked last year. I need you to put together something like that."

That one was tricky. We cut it three percent, gave them a good deal on admin fees, and barely hit our minimum.

Not to mention it took me all weekend to get that one done.

"Which company is leading?" I asked. Knowing my competition almost always helped.

"No idea. My guess is it's not as widespread as they want us to believe. Broker's probably trying to squeeze us."

The porch light came on and I looked up. Regina probably saw my car on the doorbell camera. Hopefully she had dinner ready. I was starving.

"Alright," I said. "I'll work on it tonight. Try to get you something ASAP."

"Sounds good. Just remember, if we don't feel this is a good deal, then that's cool. We just need to get them to feel the same way. It's not a good deal until *both* sides feel like they got the short end of the stick."

I'd heard him say that a dozen times. But it was so true.

"Cool. I'll send you my updates shortly."

"Appreciate you, Micah. This one's a win if we can land it. I'll be sure to bring your name up at my next exec meeting."

"I appreciate that, John."

We hung up. I sat there a minute, frustrated—

this wasn't what I had planned for the night.

But deals didn't close themselves.

Harper was represented by one of our toughest brokers. Extremely competitive with rates and wasn't afraid to test the market. I knew I had a long night ahead of me. But the plan was simple… eat dinner quick with Regina and the boys, then lock myself in the office for however long I needed to.

But when I stepped inside the house, things didn't start the way I expected. No smell of dinner drifting down the hallway—just a shadow and a dim glow coming from the living room.

Regina had her legs under the blanket, screen lighting up her face. I leaned down and kissed her on the cheek.

"Hey," I said. "You didn't cook tonight?"

She glanced up, her eyebrows pulling together. "What do you mean? Didn't you pick up the pizza?"

"Pizza?" I repeated. The word felt foreign in my mouth.

But only for a second.

Second Friday of the month. Our turn to host the small group. Seven o'clock. The same group we'd been part of for months.

"Sorry," I said, rubbing the back of my neck. "I don't know how I forgot."

"About the meeting or pizza?" she asked.

"Both."

She didn't snap. Just gave a small nod and slid her feet off the couch, reaching for her Crocs. She did let out a small sigh—just loud enough for me to feel it.

"It's okay," she said. "I'll go pick it up. Bradley's asleep upstairs and Xavier's outside with his friends. Should be coming in any minute."

She started walking toward the entryway.

And that's when the guilt hit me and I had something else to confess.

"I actually forgot to order it."

She froze mid-step and slowly turned around. Her face said it all. Tight-lipped. Narrow eyes. Trying not to let it all out at once.

Yet, she still pulled it together before speaking. "Do you think we can place an order now and it'll be ready by seven?"

I shook my head. "I doubt it. And listen…" I paused, dropping my laptop bag onto the kitchen island. "I know it's last minute but can we see if someone else can host tonight? I have to get something done for work."

She crossed her arms. "No, Micah. I'm sure some people are already on their way. This is our time to host. I'm not about to cancel on them again."

I felt her wall go up. The same wall that always showed up when work pulled me in one direction and she needed me in the other.

But there was too much pressure for me to fold.

"Fine," I huffed. "But I'm not sure how much help I can be tonight. John needs me to update this proposal tonight."

She placed her hand on her head, gathering herself before speaking.

"So, you expect me to do this entire presentation by myself? Our section is for Hebrews Six. Growing in Christ. Leaving the elementary things. Not repeating the same habits."

Every word felt like it was addressed to me.

But I wasn't going to argue with her. I knew how she felt. She just wanted connection—with me and the church. I did too. But we could do that by going to church more. These small groups were kind of a waste of time.

"Look baby, I'm sorry, but I won't be much help anyway because I haven't read the chapter… And how about we check and see if Kevin and Denise can host? They live right down the street."

"They hosted last month, Micah."

"So, they should be able to again. Just this once. I promise I'll be ready for the next one."

Her head tilted slightly like she couldn't believe what she was hearing.

"No, Micah. I already confirmed with Pastor this morning. I even texted you at twelve to remind you about everything. I'm not cancelling last minute all because you forgot to do what you're supposed to do."

I opened my mouth to get defensive but shut it again. She wasn't just upset about hosting—she was upset about me not showing up for her. For us. And I could either keep defending myself or meet her halfway.

"You're right," I said, letting out a slow exhale. "Let's figure this out... We can just order from the chain down the street—they're pretty quick if you do pickup."

"And what about you?" she asked. "You're gonna be out here with us?"

"Yeah, I should be able to knock this out in about an hour. I probably won't make it for the social part, but I'll come out before you start speaking."

She didn't reply, she just turned toward the door with tension in her steps like she was ready to storm out.

But halfway there, something seemed to hit her. Her shoulders eased, and she stopped, drawing in a breath before coming back toward me. She placed her hand on my arm, her tone softer now.

"Micah, I know your job is important, but I really need you to be more aware of everyone else. Forgetting about us is becoming a pattern. I know you don't mean to, but it still affects me and the boys."

"I got you," I said, giving her a kiss. "I'll work on being a better husband and father."

She shook her head. "You don't need to be a better husband or father. I just need you to make us a priority. Some days, you treat us like we mean the world to you… but it's just not consistent enough."

Then she turned and walked away, leaving the words to sit with me.

I stood there for a moment but tried my best to not worry. Things were going to get better soon. I just needed to spend more time with her. Maybe I'd switch my gym time to mornings instead of evenings. Take her out on a date at least once a week.

Yeah, that's what I'll do.

I pulled out my phone and opened the OpenTable app and found a slot for tomorrow at a restaurant in Addison that she'd been wanting to try. I also made a mental note to add an extra day for the nanny. That way Regina could have a day to herself during the week. She could sleep in, go out—do whatever she wanted.

I smiled and sang as I went into my home office.

I sat down and my fingers flew across the keys. Years of spreadsheets, models, and proposals had trained me for this kind of last-minute work. Adjusting formulas, tightening projections gave me a new wave of confidence.

Forty-five minutes passed like nothing.

Regina came back.

Then the doorbell rang—the Rodgers, always early. I gave them a quick wave. Jamal lingered by the office door like he wanted to say something but I kept my eyes on my computer screen. It took him a good thirty seconds to catch the hint before he finally drifted into the living room with his wife and Regina.

Then the Pastor and his wife arrive.

Then everyone else.

They all chatted, laughed and ate while I wrapped up my exhibits.

Thirty minutes after that, I was done—or least thought I was. I gave John a call.

"Micah," he answered quick, like he'd been waiting. "What you got for me?"

"I was able to cut the rate by four percent without sacrificing margin," I boasted. "I also adjusted our admin fee, giving a little more room for BAFO."

I clicked a few buttons on the Zoom call and shared my screen. John was silent for a minute or two, then came the magic words.

"Good work, Micah."

I smiled. He actually sounded proud. And not just because I pulled it off, but because I thought ahead. I did something others wouldn't have been able to do.

"You took initiative," he added. "I didn't have to walk you through anything. You saw the opportunity, moved smart, and protected our margin. Good job. Go ahead and type up the email and send it to the broker. CC me on it. I'll review it tonight just in case... but honestly, it looks like you nailed it."

"Thanks, John. I appreciate it."

"No—thank you. If this deal closes, your name's going to come up in all the right circles. Trust me."

We exchanged a few more words before ending the call. For a moment after, I just sat there staring at the screen, admiring my work.

Then Regina tapped on the door.

"Micah, are you joining us?"

She hit me with one of those play-it-cool voices. If company wasn't here, it wouldn't have been as nice.

"Yeah, just a sec," I said, avoiding eye contact. "I'll be right out once I send this email."

She pulled the door closed with just enough force to let me know how she felt.

I opened my email, attached the new files, and began typing the message to the broker. As I hovered over the send button, I overheard Regina covering for me when Larry asked what I was doing.

I felt bad.

But John called back before I could react. "Hey, before you send, I noticed that you didn't include the financial summary. Be sure to attach that."

"Ok, I will," I said.

Only problem—I hadn't even done one for this account.

It took me nearly an hour to create one. And finally, I hit send without checking over what I typed. I was exhausted.

I stepped out of the office and into the kitchen. The smell of garlic and tomato sauce lingered in the air. The pizza boxes were pushed to one side of the kitchen counter, half-empty. Everyone was gathered in a circle in the living room, already deep into the study.

I smiled as I passed, trying not to draw too much attention. I put a slice of pepperoni and then cheese onto my plate and sat in the kitchen alone. Close enough to hear them, but far enough to not be fully part of it just yet.

Regina's voice flowed smoothly. *"Not laying again the foundation of repentance from dead works and of faith toward God."*

It was more than presenting—her words sounded personal. Like she had lived this lesson.

I chimed in when Kevin mentioned spiritual

growth requiring discomfort.

"I think that's what makes growth tough. We want *the* change but sometimes don't want *to* change."

Regina glanced over at me, then back at the group. It was hard to read her expression. Maybe she was upset that I just chimed in, or maybe she was like 'About time.' Either way, I didn't get the reaction I expected.

After eating, I stayed at the table. When Regina finished her lesson, everyone told her how good of a job she'd done. She lit up.

Around ten, everyone had gone home. Regina and I cleaned up and climbed in bed shortly after.

"Good job," I said, rubbing her arm. "Sorry, I wasn't in there with you the whole time, but it didn't look like I needed to anyway."

She moved her arm closer to her body. I had my hand stretched just enough to still touch her. "Micah, it's not about needing you. I *wanted* you in there with me. But as always, they needed you more."

"I know and I'm sorry," I said. "John really pushed for the exhibits tonight. But good news is—they'll probably accept the bid."

"And what does that do for you?"

I chuckled, surprised she'd even ask that. "Everything. Steve, our CEO, is a direct contact to this firm. If I win it, best believe I'd get an email from him."

"And what does that do for you?" she repeated, this time with a sharper tone in her voice.

My brows furrowed. "What do you mean what

does that do for me? It means that the most important guy in the company would know who I am."

She slightly pulled her arm away. Not enough to where we weren't touching anymore, but enough to let me know she didn't want to be.

"What's wrong?" I asked, shifting my demeanor from excited to concerned.

She took a breath. "Micah, now might not be the right time to say this… but I'm not happy. I haven't been happy in a long time."

Her words hit me like a head-on collision.

She wasn't happy? How could she not be when she has everything she's asked for? She's the one who picked out this house, and that Mercedes out front. I was driving her old Nissan. I even allowed her to turn the movie room into her little she-space—that she never uses.

And now that I'm about to close a big deal, she tells me she's not happy?

"Regina where is this coming from?" I barked. "I thought things were better since we moved. Matter of fact, you just told me a couple weeks ago that you love Dallas."

She let out a frustrated chuckle, shaking her head.

"Dallas is great Micah. But I don't sleep next to Dallas at night. And I don't raise kids with Dallas."

My nostrils flared. *How dare her snap on me like that?*

"So, everything I'm doing doesn't matter, huh?"

She sat up, taking a second before answering my question. "That's not what I said, Micah. What I'm saying is a new city may have changed our location but it hasn't changed us."

"What do you mean it hasn't changed us? We haven't even argued since we been here."

"And you think that's normal?" she asked, crossing her arms. "Or do you think we don't argue because I decided to keep quiet and you decided to not care."

I felt those words in my chest. But it wasn't anger now. It was that shaky feeling I used to get when we'd argue—when I didn't have the words to defend myself.

But how did we even get here? I thought we had an effective strategy. I grind while she holds the house down. Do I work late sometimes? Yeah. But doesn't she go out with the women in our small group? Where is this sudden unhappiness coming from?

"Listen, Regina, I do care. But if you're asking me to stop working so much, then tell me how. You gonna help me find another job? Or are you ready to get one yourself? Because there aren't many jobs out here paying what I make now."

She shook her head, rolling her eyes like I missed the point. "Micah, it's not about how much you work. It's about the times when you're here that bothers me. We try to watch movies and you're checking emails. We go out, but you're taking phone calls. I can never get alone time with you."

Tears rolled down her face. I was about to reach for her, but I froze. *What was I going to say?* That I was sorry? That I'd do better? Regina wasn't trying to hear any of that.

And honestly, I didn't see anything wrong with working so much. At least I wasn't out running the streets. I was home every night. Never cheated, didn't hang out with the fellas. If anything, I should be offended. Here I am working hard and she says she's not happy.

Maybe she needs to meet John and see what a non-present husband looks like. He's been married for twenty years and doesn't even like his wife. It shows. He purposely stays at work just to avoid going home.

I took a deep breath so the words boiling in my chest wouldn't slip out. Matching her energy wouldn't fix this.

"How can I make this better?" I asked. "I'll do anything you want me to."

She let out a heavy sigh. "Let's just go to sleep."

"Regina…"

She ignored me and slid down from the headboard and rolled onto her stomach, burying her face in the pillow.

"Goodnight, Micah," was all she said.

I stood there in the dark, watching her back, realizing silence wasn't just silence anymore.

It was distance.

And tonight, it felt permanent.

CHAPTER SEVEN

"So, you really think she's right?" I bellowed. "A man who works his butt off for his family is a problem now? Wow."

I leaned back and rested an elbow against the door panel. I no longer cared what Lior thought. This is exactly why I kept people out of my business. How could he possibly be on her side? How did he have the nerve to call me out over a missed Bible study lesson and say small groups are just as important as church?

Well, guess what, Lior? Missing that lesson is what landed that client. And I still made it to church that Sunday and got a good word.

The only downside was that Regina was mad for a few nights. But even that passed. Especially after I took her to that restaurant.

Lior answered my question. "Micah, I never said a working man is a problem."

"You might as well have," I seethed. "You think I'm not a good man because I'm not out there playing Uno with the boys every night—or because I'm not sitting through some fake TV show with Regina?"

Lior placed his hand on his forehead. "Do you really think Uno's the goal? Or watching a show? Or could there be a deeper reasoning behind it all?"

I chuckled. Lior was all questions with no answers. He challenges but doesn't give true advice. Yeah… he was definitely a screwup back in the day. No other way to explain it.

He didn't understand the weight I carried. The trade-offs I made. The long nights I'd stayed up working for them.

"Lior, look—the only goal is to provide. How can I provide for them if I'm playing games or gathering with friends every night? Did you miss the part when I said *all* of them church folk who want to meet up all the time are broke? I've even lent a couple of them money."

"Micah…" he said quietly. "Provision isn't just money. Who's pouring into your kids? Who's making them smile? Or is that just Regina's responsibility?"

"Watch yourself," I warned. "You don't know me like that to judge me or my wife."

Lior glanced out the window. Not upset, not happy—just that same face I couldn't read.

Or deal with.

This time, I was serious about dropping him off. Next gas station I see, he's out. I was tired of playing the polite driver. There was no sign of Jordan Heights and he was wearing me out with his half-parables and quiet stares. I didn't have the energy to sit and decode every riddle. My plate was already full and I still needed to prep for this meeting. I thought I'd have time to recite a few lines, run the numbers in my head, but I was stuck playing cab driver to an ungrateful stranger.

Let him preach to someone else. Maybe the next person's life was messed up. Mine wasn't... I was doing good—better than most.

"Looks like you're trying to convince yourself something," he blurted out, as if he could read my mind.

I kept my eyes straight. "Not really. Just hoping I find a restaurant or gas station soon."

"Hungry?"

"Nope. Just need to stop."

He didn't ask a follow-up. I wouldn't have told him anyway. He'd find out once I looked him in his eyes and told him this was where our journey together ends.

I focused on the road. Nothing but trees and wire fences stretched for miles, each one reminding me how far I was from where I thought I'd be by now.

A few miles later, houses appeared in the distance. One had a rusted basketball goal leaning sideways. Another had a screen door flapping in the wind.

We were getting close to something.

I slowed down a bit.

Still, I said nothing—and neither did he. But I could feel him watching me again.

Moments later, he looked out at the open grass fields for a moment, then picked the conversation back up.

"Sometimes we confuse survival with service. You keep saying you're doing it for them, but it sounds more like you're doing it so you don't feel like a failure. Nonstop work while your wife's lonely."

My shoulders rose as I drew in a deep breath. "I think it's best we just stop talking to each other."

"And why is that?" he jabbed. "Is it because I said your wife is lonely?"

My jaw clenched and my eyes narrowed. *Did he really just say that?*

He did.

I yanked the wheel, pulled over, slammed the gear into park, and turned to him. Heat shot through me, similar to how it did my senior year in high school when Dwayne fouled me. That was the only fight I'd ever been into my life, and this moment felt like it was about to go down the same way.

"Look," I said, pointing my finger at him. "You can say whatever about me all you want, but keep my wife's name out your mouth. You don't know anything about her."

He stared me down, unfazed. "Feels like a mirror, doesn't it?"

I leaned back slightly, my anger transitioning to confusion. "What… what are you talking about?"

A smile broke. "Tell me one thing about what I just said that you hadn't said yourself?"

I shook my head. "I never told you she was lonely. I said she complains. Big difference."

"Correct," he replied, his eyebrows lifting. "You never told *me*, but how many times have you told yourself?"

I ran my hand over my face. "Look, enough with the games. She's not lonely. She's just—something. Maybe in a season of… complaining, I guess. Nothing I do is ever good enough."

"You ever ask yourself why?"

"I'm not answering that, man. I told you I'm not talking to you anymore. How far are we from the next town?"

Lior looked at the trees. "I thought you knew where you were going. When we were at that fork, you veered right."

"That's because you didn't tell me which way," I snapped. "Enough of these games, already."

Lior got quiet. As always.

I checked the time and it was a little past nine. Already late based on my standards.

I threw the gear into drive and stomped on the pedal, jerking back onto the road without even checking my mirrors. My anger was running the wheel, not me.

We drove for a good thirty minutes in silence. But it wasn't true silence. Tensed. My hands stayed locked on the wheel, knuckles tight. Every few seconds, I'd shift my grip, feeling nervous like something was going different than it should.

I was too tired to keep going back and forth with him. Too tired to keep trying to prove my point. Why argue with someone who really didn't know me? He didn't know about those nights early in our marriage when I came home and skipped dinner so Regina and

Xavier could eat. How I used to stare at the gas pump, praying my card wouldn't decline. How I used to beg for money from friends. How I spent nights thinking I was becoming my father.

Now my family had stability. Regina didn't have to clock in and come home exhausted. I gave her peace. Freedom. And yeah, I was still learning how to show up emotionally—but that didn't make me a failure.

Rain tapped across the windshield, steady and insistent, like fingers drumming for my attention. I flipped the wipers up a notch.

Then suddenly, the clouds thinned. Just a sliver of light at first, then a brighter crack in the gray.

And there it was—

A faint arc stretching across the sky ahead. Not a full rainbow, but full enough to stop me mid-thought.

The sight reached into me before I had a chance to fight it. A covenant. A reminder. The tension in my chest loosened, just slightly, like the rainbow had pulled the weight off my thoughts for a second.

I turned to Lior. He was staring at the same rainbow. Then I thought about it. Maybe I was a little harsh.

I thought about apologizing—but no… that would make me look weak. It wasn't just about pride, but I had a decision to execute. I was still dropping him off at the next town and didn't want my apology to be mistaken for an invitation to stay.

I had an internal debate for miles. I was a compassionate man. Something about me dropping him off didn't feel right. What if I needed him?

Then, he said something.

"Micah, what really drives you?"

I didn't want to answer his question but did anyway.

"I told you. Making sure I give my kids the life I never had."

No follow up, no nod, just staring ahead.

I smirked, ready to flip it on him this time. "Alright, your turn," I said. "When you're not hitching rides or handing out *advice*, what drives you?"

"Jesus."

I waited for more.

Nothing.

"That's it?" I asked, a slight chuckle in my voice. "Not saying that's wrong but what *really* drives you? People say God or Jesus all the time yet their minds are focused on other things."

"Not me."

"So... you just what... pray all day?"

He grinned. "No, Micah, I do a lot of things. I fish, teach people how to fish... and I build things— but that's not what you asked. You asked what drives me. So yes, it's always the Almighty Lord."

I gave a slow nod, more out of obligation than agreement. "Alright, preacher man. Tell me about fishing then?"

He raised his arms slightly. "Nothing really to it. I just go out and fish sometimes. And if I see people struggling, I teach them."

I wasn't sure it that was literal—or just another

metaphor.

"Ever been married?" I asked.

"No."

I grinned. "See, that's what separates you and me. Only men with families understands the weight that comes with it. You give great advice Lior, but you have to understand a man before you judge them."

No response.

I smiled on the inside. Finally, he didn't have a comeback. It was easy for him to talk when he'd never been in my shoes. Didn't have a wife and kids to provide for.

A notification from my phone broke through the silence. I looked down and saw the screen light up in the cup holder. I grabbed it quickly.

It was an email from John about my colleague, Sean Thomas. He'd just closed the Johnson deal. Second biggest deal of the year. Nowhere near my wins, but he always got more credit.

I exhaled hard and let the phone fall back into the holder.

And then it hit me—I had service!

I snatched it up again, finger hitting the Maps icon. The screen spun, then locked onto a blue dot.

Right on course. Not as early as I wanted, but I'd still get there before eleven. Maybe enough time to check in, shower and head across the street for the meeting.

Minutes later, the sky began to clear even more. Then a dusty sign for a gas station came into view. Shiloh Stop 2 miles.

That's it. That's where I'll drop Lior off. That'll give me time to recite my pitch and maybe call Regina. Let her know about this weird day.

I slowed down once I saw it. A little doubt but it still felt right.

Lior looked over at the gas station—almost as if he knew the place. That made me feel better. He'd be okay. Could probably find a ride from someone else.

I parked near the pump and let the car idle. For a few seconds, I didn't move. I just sat there, staring at the cracked paint on the building and thinking through my next move. My mind was already shifting gears—trying to push past whatever Lior had stirred up and get into game mode.

I reached down and hit the unlock button. *Click.*

Lior turned to me, his voice calm and steady. "Well. I guess this is where I get out, eh?"

I looked in his direction but kept my eyes straight ahead. "Yeah… Sorry. I just—I just need to get my head together before this meeting. You think you'll be okay?"

"Yes, I will," he said with a nod. "I understand. Truly. You've taken us as far as you can. Thank you."

I tried not to dwell on it, but the way he said *"as far as you can"* stuck with me.

"You're welcome. Take care, Lior."

He touched my shoulder and that same divine or angelic feeling surged through me again—this time stronger.

He opened the door slowly but didn't step out right away. He looked around once, as if he was taking in the setting. Then he turned back to me with a warm expression.

"This is it for now. I will see you down the road."

I forced a smile. "Yeah…"

But in my head? *Nah. This is it.*

He stepped out and closed the door behind him.

I shifted into drive, let the tires roll forward, and didn't look back.

CHAPTER EIGHT

Finally, peace and quiet, and a working phone.

I merged back onto the main road, preparing for the final stretch of my journey. I couldn't lie, I felt bad for parting ways with Lior, but he was just jumping on subjects that he knew nothing about. Maybe if we talked sports, or even politics, we could've gotten better ground.

I glanced back just before the store disappeared. No sign of him. He'd either gone inside or already caught another ride. Either way, it wasn't my problem.

My GPS broke through my thoughts. *In a quarter mile, turn right.*

The robotic voice filled the car, and for once, it felt like music. Finally, no judgment, just guidance.

I nodded, like the voice was talking to me directly. "Okay," I whispered. "I'll turn right."

At ten o'clock sharp, my phone lit up. John. I tapped the screen, answering through Bluetooth.

"Hey, John," I said, sounding more cheerful than I had all morning.

"Hey. Just wanted to check in with you before your meeting. I meant to call you back yesterday. How was the flight in?"

"I actually drove," I replied. "Didn't want to stick around to see if they were going to cancel the flight."

"Smart," he said. I could hear the smile in his voice. "When'd you get in?"

I hesitated. "I'm actually not there yet—but almost. Should be there in about thirty minutes or so."

He paused another second or two. Just enough for me to sense his displeasure.

"Why aren't you there yet? You do know the meeting starts in an hour, right?"

My hands tightened around the steering wheel. I wasn't afraid of him, but since I respected him, I gave him the quick rundown.

"Last night I stopped in a small town and a storm broke out while I was there. I stayed the night, then had a couple hiccups this morning. But don't worry, sir, I'll get there on time."

I waited for the usual "good job" or at least some kind of approval. Instead, his voice cut sharp like he was talking to a five-year-old who wandered off in the grocery store.

"You can't just make decisions like that, Micah. Matter of fact, did you even call Lisa to cancel the flight?"

"Not yet, but I will after the meeting."

"Don't even bother," he sighed. "It's too late for a refund anyway. You should've called her as soon as you decided to drive."

I eased off the gas, shaking my head. *Well, excuse me for trying to take initiative.* I had a head full of steam. Was he really blaming me? I'd driven here on my own dime, paid for my own motel, my own gas—well, Lior took care of the gas, but still. The company hadn't spent a penny besides the flight.

"John listen—"

"No, I need you to listen," he cut me off. "You're supposed to lead by example. You've had since yesterday and you're still not there. What if something else happens and you get there late? I can tell you now… that won't be a good look. We can't afford to lose this deal. That's why I chose you… but honestly, I'm starting to feel like I made a mistake."

My eyes widened as his words landed. John could be direct sometimes, but never really had that kind of tone with me.

Despite the anger boiling up, I bit my tongue. At least for now. Maybe I'd call him out in our next team meeting—but not today. John had enough on his plate. The higher-ups were already breathing down his neck, and everyone knows how pressure rolls downhill. He was a good dude. Just a good dude under a lot of stress.

"John, I hear you," I said quietly, the words dragging out of me painfully. "Don't worry—I'll be there on time."

"I hope so," he said, tone still sharp. "If not, call me ASAP. I'll have to make up something and get Sean to do a Zoom call with them."

I took a slow breath, because I was about to respond in a way that could really jeopardize my job. There was no way I'd give Sean this account back.

"Look," I said carefully. "I don't see myself being late, but worst case, I'll pull over and do a Zoom call with them myself. Explain what happened. But with all due respect, Sean doesn't have the experience for this and you know it."

I breathed in a little confidence after saying what I said. I didn't raise my voice. Didn't try to sound defensive. I just stated facts.

But John went a different direction with his next comment.

"Look Micah. Things are pretty tight this quarter. Our budget is slipping. You're already on the top half of the salary spectrum. I really need you to be on time and close every deal you get your hands on. I don't want to get into too many details so I'll just leave it at that."

I stared at the highway like it was the one who just threatened my job.

So, that's what this was about. Numbers. I was one of the longest tenured employees and almost at the *new* salary cap. They had no problem with reminding me that.

And I had no problem with proving my worth.

"John, you don't have to worry about anything," I said. "I *will* be there. And I *will* close this deal."

He seemed unfazed by my determination. "Just call me when you get there so I know when I can relax."

The phone went dead.

I let out a deep breath. So, that's how he's gonna end the call with his top employee? All those nights I choked down vending machine sandwiches just to keep the numbers moving. All those times Regina texted, *you almost home?* and I lied just to buy myself more time at the office?

And why bring up my salary like it's some kind of burden? I've been solid. Loyal in ways they don't even value no more. I didn't ask for the spotlight—I just showed up. Took the hard accounts, the unreasonable clients. Closed deals from parking lots and hospital rooms. I've pitched proposals in my car while my wife was inside the mall shopping. Even on holidays. Last Christmas Eve, I was sitting in the car fixing someone else's mess.

And somehow that still wasn't enough.

What really bothers me is that I didn't even flinch when my flight got canceled. I just made the decision to drive. Didn't wait for instructions, didn't whine. I *moved.*

A sign appeared, pointing to the right for Jordan Heights. I thought about turning but the GPS told me to keep straight. I wasn't familiar with the town so maybe their office was on the outskirts.

My phone rang. For a second, I thought it was John again, but when I saw the name, my chest eased.

Regina!

I answered quickly. "Hey, sweetheart. I was just about to call you."

"Hey," she said, her voice still laced with sleepiness. "Did you make it in?"

"Not yet. I'm about fifteen minutes out. It's been a crazy morning. Left at five, drove through a storm and all."

"Wow, you left that early?" she asked, suddenly more alert. "Why didn't you call me when you left the motel?"

"I tried but didn't have service."

"Did you buy a map?"

I chuckled. "Nah. I gave this guy a ride and just dropped him off about an hour ago. He really got on my nerves, but honestly, he knew where he was going and showed me most of the way."

She sucked in a sharp breath. "Micah, are you serious? You picked up a stranger? Don't you watch the news? Anything could've happened to you."

"I know, I know," I said quickly. "But he actually helped me. I never would've made it this far—without him."

"Still," she muttered. "You gotta stop doing stuff like that. It's dangerous out here."

I let out a soft chuckle, but it faded quickly. Her voice had that edge to it. Something seemed off. But I didn't want to press, so I reached for softer ground.

"So, how'd you sleep?"

"Not good."

"Why not?"

Silence at first. Then she said softly, "I feel like— I'm losing you, Micah. I try not to complain but trying to hold it down all the time hurts. I'm happy for you but I don't know if I can live like this anymore. Please don't take it the wrong way. I'm just… tired."

Her words lingered, causing a funny feeling in my chest. Tired? Again? We'd just went through this not too long ago. What did this woman want from me?

And as always, I searched for the right thing to say—something to hurry up and get rid of whatever she was feeling.

"I get it honey. I've been putting in a lot of work while you've been home. But this will probably be one of the last times I have to travel. John already said my salary is too high for this position so I'm sure they're ready to promote me."

She let out a frustrated chuckle. "You really think that's what that means, Micah? Did you not forget all the other things you've said they've done? Can't you see you're just a number?"

I smacked my teeth. "I'm too valuable for them to let me go. John called a few minutes ago and was upset—but I think it was more so because he's putting in a good word for me and doesn't want himself to look bad. Trust me, they wouldn't let me go. Not after everything I've done for them."

Even I didn't believe what I'd just said. But I still had to be confident to Regina.

For a moment, we both went quiet. I passed another sign. White background—letters blurred too fast to catch. I tried looking back, but it was gone.

The road stretched empty again. No cars. No sound besides the hum of my tires.

I checked my phone to make sure the call was

still connected. It was. I could almost picture her on the other end of the line… sitting on the edge of the bed, staring off into space. Or her AirPods in and playing a game on her phone.

Then she finally spoke.

"Micah…" she said, and something in her tone made me listen carefully. "I had a dream… it felt too real. In it, you left the house… kind of like the other morning. Later, you called, said you closed some deal and got the promotion and were on your way home. But when you got here, somehow the house turned into our old apartment back in Atlanta."

She paused, and my chest tightened. I had no idea where this was going.

"I could hear you trying to get in. We could talk through the door, clear as day. You were telling me all these good things about the deal. How it was gonna fulfill you. Make you happy. I pulled on the door and the knob broke off, and it still wouldn't open. Then my hands started bleeding. I was being cut by the key I didn't even know I was holding. Then I dropped it… and woke up."

I didn't say anything right away. Just sat there, letting her words settle. I asked God silently for interpretation.

Seconds later, it hit me out of nowhere.

Maybe I'd been home in the physical sense—but not in the way it mattered. And Regina… she'd been holding the key the whole time. Willing to open the door. Willing to fight for us. Bleeding for the marriage. And me? I had my hand on the knob, stopping it from turning.

And then it broke off.

"Listen, we can fix this," I cried. "I'll come home right after the meeting and take a few days off. I'll see if Shawna can watch the boys."

There was a pause. Long enough for me to picture her deciding whether or not to let me off the hook. My heart thudded with quiet desperation. I needed her to believe me. Needed her to feel how serious I was.

But her voice came back sharp. "You can't always fix things, Micah. This isn't work. I'm not a client you can just manage into submission. I'm not something that snaps back into place just because you said the right words. That's not who I am anymore."

Her words stung, cutting me deep. For once, I didn't have control here. My throat went dry, and I scrambled for the only thing that felt safe to offer.

"I'll just—I'll just come home right now," I said. "Forget this meeting. Let's talk about this when I get there."

"No," she said quickly. "There's nothing to talk about. Like I said, you can't just fix things, Micah. I'm tired of this."

"And what's that supposed to mean?"

She didn't answer right away, and the silence made the question louder.

"You just don't get it, Micah. You keep thinking if you just show up and say the right thing, it'll be okay. But I'm tired. This isn't something that's just started bothering me. It's been that way for a while.

You don't know how many nights I've cried, asking God why should I stay in this marriage when all he cares about is work. I tried to fight the feeling… but I just can't no more."

I rested my hand on my thigh, tapping without rhythm. I didn't like where this was headed. I could feel the guilt creeping in, and I wanted to stop it before it took over.

"Listen, I can turn around right now," I declared. "I'll just call John and tell him I couldn't make it. If I get fired, I get fired. I don't want to lose you. I'll do whatever it takes."

She chuckled. A quick one but definitely had impact.

"I don't want you to fight for me when I'm already fed up. You should've fought for me when I was hungry for your attention."

That hit harder than anything she'd ever said.

I had no defense. Most of our marriage, I'd been afraid to lose her, but not bold enough to keep her. Keep her happy. Keep her safe.

Still, I was too invested to give up just like that.

"Baby, what can I do," I pleaded. "I hate seeing you like this. You gotta let me fix this."

"Micah, you couldn't even fix the sink," she shot back. "I had to find a video just to figure it out myself. And I'm the one who has to go to the store later to get the part. Oh… and to get the fertilizer since you don't seem to care that the grass is dead. Deader than…" She stopped herself, but the damage was already done. I knew exactly what she wanted to say.

"Regina—"

"I don't want to hear it, Micah. It's so many things I can say right now but I'm not. I can't deal with this right now."

Something in me snapped. Why was she being so cold?

"You're really being unfair," I said. "I've been doing everything I can out here to provide for y'all. Trying to keep things together. And look what you do when I'm home? Just on your phone scrolling all day."

"So, that's what you think I do all day?" she asked in a low but serious voice.

I felt bad, but I was tired of always biting my tongue. She gets to tell me she's tired but I don't get to tell her how I feel? Nope, not today.

"Yes," I said, tone firmer than I'd been with her in years. "All you do is complain and spend my money. I go to work, deal with crap and can't even come home to a cooked meal every day. You're tired? Maybe I'm tired too."

The line got quiet. And I got nervous. I almost wished she would've cut me off.

But when her voice returned, it was calm. Too calm.

"Micah, I'm done."

"Done with what?"

"Everything," she sighed. "I'll figure out where me and the boys gonna go. But you just proved you don't care about me or what I go through. And I'm tired—tired of explaining it, tired of swallowing my problems because everyone thinks you're the good guy. But I don't care anymore. One day, you'll realize what you had."

Then the line went dead.

I thought about calling her back but it wouldn't do any good. I even thought about turning around, but we've been through rough patches before. Not to take light of it but I had other things to worry about. I'll just buy her some flowers, talk to her and fix things. Really fix them this time.

I drove straight for a few miles, mind focused on the meeting. Suddenly, I saw something that made me slam on brakes. Barricades and a sign bright as day— 'Road Closed'.

Just beyond it—open road. But no detour. No alternate route.

I stared at the GPS. Still said to go straight. Still showed a clean blue line like I was right on track.

I got a close to it as I could, let the engine idle for a second. Frozen in disbelief. I had ten minutes left according to GPS, but no way to go through.

I put the car in park and stepped out. Walked up to the barricades. Looked like they'd been there for a while. Like someone fixed a pothole and decided to just leave the road closed.

Then I thought about it. That sign I passed while on the phone with Regina—maybe it was a warning or a detour.

But that was miles ago. No other turns in between. And if I did turn around, I wouldn't make it in time.

For the first time in a long time, I had no one but myself to blame for this.

Not Regina.

Not John.

Not the airline.

Not even Lior.

Just me.

Alone on a road where I missed the signs.

CHAPTER NINE

I knocked on John's door and waited, already bracing myself. I knew what I wanted to say, but wasn't sure how to say it.

"Come in."

I opened the door and stepped in quietly. He was just hanging up a phone call. He glanced at me with that aggravated look—like either something had already gone wrong, or my presence alone was enough to annoy him.

"Got a minute?" I asked, stepping inside fully.

He motioned for me to sit. "Yeah, but make it quick," he said, keeping his eyes on the computer screen. "Kinda in the middle of something."

I cleared my throat. "Ok… I wanted to ask about the promotion. I overheard some chatter—sounds like a decision's already been made."

He stopped typing abruptly and looked up, eyebrows slightly raised. "Who'd you hear that from?"

I hesitated, not wanting to throw Tim and David under the bus. They were good people—but they did gossip too much.

"I just overheard some people talking at lunch," I said. "Not really sure who it was."

He leaned back in his chair, rubbed his chin, and let out a sigh. Whatever urgency he had a minute ago was gone.

"So, I'm guessing you know who it is too, huh?"

"If it's true what I heard—yeah."

He rubbed his eyes, keeping his hands there for a few extra seconds. "Micah, just so you know, it was close. I know you wanted it… but we had to look at the big picture. Sean has had more exposure on bigger accounts, and because of that, his name has come up more often in conversations with senior leadership."

I breathed a heavy sigh. Knowing it was Sean who got the promotion was one thing, but hearing it from John—that was a different kind of sting.

"But I trained him," I shot back. "Showed him everything he knows. Matter of fact, he still comes to me for questions. You do know that was my old presentation that he used in our last team meeting, right?"

"I know and thank you," John said with his head lowered. "Like I said, it was close. But when Tony sat in Sean's last presentation, the first thing he said after was that he's taking after his dad."

Of course he was. His dad was Michael Thomas, VP of Sales. I should've known when they hired him straight out of college and put him in my department, he'd be trouble for me.

Sean already had his own office. It took years for me to get mine. He skipped the waiting game that I had to play. No extra hours, no relocating, just walked in and basically said, 'I'm Michael's son.' And just like that, doors opened.

"So, they just overlooked me because I don't have a dad who works in senior leadership," I said, letting out a frustrated chuckle. "Oh, and by the way, I've been with the company longer than his dad."

John lifted his chin and formed a sheepish grin. Just before speaking, he looked out the door to make sure no one was nearby.

"Micah, I can see why you feel that way. Work ethic—you've been solid. No one can question that. It really boils down to visibility. Sean shows up to all the events hosted by leadership. He volunteers, attends happy hours and he's always early for meetings—just to mingle."

Of course, you can be early for meetings if you're just sitting at your desk not doing anything. John, Megan and Christy still sends him leads. Me, on the other hand—I'm always out in the field doing the hard work.

I threw my hands up. "So, I guess it's not about the money I bring in or how dedicated I am, I should just make sure I volunteer to make blankets and care packets—oh and drink cheap liquor with all the rich guys. That'll get me promoted, huh?"

John shot me a look. One that basically said I didn't have a right to be upset about this. Well, I did have the right. Because this was my second time applying for this role and second time being turned down. The last dude they selected isn't even with the company anymore.

"Micah," John said slowly. "You have to understand that it's more than doing a good job. I admit it's not fair, but they are looking for a people's person. Someone who socializes—in and outside of the office."

"I have a family at home," I vented. "Look, I already told you how Regina gets when I stay at work late. You really think I can tell her that I have to go to happy hours? You want me to sleep on the couch?"

John chuckled but straightened his face quickly once he saw that I wasn't smiling.

He took off his glasses and placed his elbows on the table. "Micah, I get it—but those events aren't just social, they're strategic. You'd be surprised how much gets decided off the clock. We're busy working during regular hours. The people who show up at the events are the ones who get noticed the most."

He let his words hang in the air a moment before continuing.

"I know you can't go to all the events… Even Sean has missed a few. But you haven't been to not one social event this year."

"That's because I barely drink. And besides, none of you have little kids at home or live as far as I do."

John paused. He shifted his chair, turned and looked at the calendar on his wall—tapping his fingers as if he was cooking up something.

"Alright, Micah," he said after a few moments, flashing a smile. "What's done is done. How about I do something else for you? An opportunity. It comes with a guaranteed bonus—and might even lead to a better promotion than this one."

I leaned in, trying to see what was circled on his calendar but couldn't see it clearly.

"Like what?"

John nodded slowly. "I have an opportunity for one of—if not the biggest deal of the year. But it's in Jordan Heights and you'll have to fly out tomorrow."

I blinked, trying to read his expression. "Jordan Heights? Why me? Is this a new deal?"

His eyes shot up to the door again, then back at me. He leaned forward, lowered his tone. "Between me and you… this was Sean's client, but it's stalled. I want to send you because I know you'll get the job done."

I looked at him for a second, trying to see where this was going. They gave Sean the promotion, but sending me to clean up his mess? Is that what they thought of me?

But before I could say anything, another thought crept in. "Wait a minute," I said. "Isn't the company party on Thursday? That was the one event I was actually planning to go to."

He hesitated. Not long—just long enough for me to know he was editing his words.

"I know," he said, looking toward his computer screen. "But there'll be more of those. There's only one deal in Jordan Heights and you're the man for it."

I lifted my eyebrow in suspicion. John always looked me in the eye—spoke with confidence. There was definitely something strange about this.

"You expect me to be able to learn this client and close a deal in two days?" I asked. "Would it be better if maybe Sean comes with me?"

John shook his head. "No. They're pretty fed up with him honestly. Listen, if it was up to me, I would've given this client to you from the jump. And this promotion would be yours. You're right about everything. Sean doesn't have the experience with a client of this size. I know you'll go there and get the deal done."

For a second, I wondered if this was just so Sean could enjoy the spotlight at the party without me around.

But I forced that thought aside. They wouldn't do that. Not John. He was sending me because he knows I'm reliable. Trusted. If this really was the biggest deal of the year, of course they'd want the right person in place.

"Alright," I said. "I'll go."

John flashed a quick, wide smile. He leaned back in his chair, exhaling like a man who'd just slipped out of an argument he didn't want to have. Almost like he was surprised that I agreed so easily.

Nah, he was just proud I handled the setback well.

He rose to his feet. "Awesome. I'll get Lisa on it so she can book you a flight. Be on the lookout for an email tonight."

I shook his hand. "Thanks, John. I'll let you get back to your work."

I walked out with a smile on my face.

But as soon as I got to my office, my heart sank.

My son was having an award ceremony tomorrow. And I promised Regina I'd be there.

For a moment, I just sat at my desk, staring at nothing. I'd known about the ceremony for weeks, even promised him I'd let him leave school early and we'd go to his favorite fast-food spot.

And now what? Tell him and Regina I'm hopping on a flight instead? I knew exactly how this would go—the job wins again.

I pressed my fingers to my temples and leaned back. Part of me wanted to march back into John's office and tell him I can't do it. But what would that change? They'd just send Sean, and I'd be the guy who passed up the biggest opportunity of the year to sit in an auditorium.

Besides, Xavier knew I loved him. Regina knew it too. I didn't have to prove my love to them. But I did have to show my worth to the company. John was doing me a favor with this. This could be the moment that would shift everything.

I'll go to Jordan Heights.

But also, to his award ceremony.

I called John. "Hey, can you ask Lisa to book a late flight?"

"There's only two flights per day going out of DFW," he said. "One at six a.m. and the other at two p.m. I recommend getting the early one just in case something happens."

I thought about it for a second. DFW was one of

the biggest and busiest airports in the country, but usually smooth. Multiple security checkpoints, multiple terminals, plenty of gates, and I'd never had a serious delay there.

"I think I'll be fine with the afternoon one," I told him. "I have to go somewhere with the fam tomorrow."

"Alright," Micah," he said with a warning in his voice. "Please, just make this flight."

"I will. Thanks, John."

I hung up. Excited. I was not only going to close this deal, I was going to be there for my family. Who says you can't do both?

*　　　*　　　*

"Where are you going, Micah?" Regina asked, stopping at the sight of my suitcase on the bed.

"I have to take an emergency trip tomorrow." I tried acting chill, mentally preparing myself for when she overreacts.

She walked closer, looking at the clothes. "Where and for what?"

I kept my reply simple. "Jordan Heights. Meeting with a client."

"And you're just now finding out about it?"

"Pretty much. John told me earlier but Lisa just sent over the itinerary before you came home."

She stood there for a second, shaking her head in disbelief. "Did you forget about Zay's—"

"No, I didn't," I cut her off gently. "I'll still be

there. My flight doesn't leave until two. His ceremony is at ten so I should be good."

She placed her hand on her forehead. "Micah, just because it starts at *ten* doesn't mean he'll be out at that time. Look, if you're on a time crunch, you might as well not even come. Better to disappoint him now than have him expect you to be there."

"It'll be fine, honey," I cheesed, waving her concern off like it was nothing. "I just need to get to the airport at least thirty minutes early. Shouldn't be too many people there that time of day."

"So, I guess you forgot about taking him to Burger Haven, huh?"

"No, I didn't forget." I gave a quick smile, hoping to defuse the edge in her voice. "Maybe you can take him. Or we'll all go this weekend."

"Whatever, Micah."

She walked downstairs, and I followed. When she sat down in the living room, I sat next to her.

"Regina, I don't want to go just as bad as you don't want me to. But John handpicked me for this. Said I'll have a good shot at getting promoted if I can land this client."

Her brows furrowed. "Didn't you just interview for a promotion two weeks ago?"

I exhaled, knowing it was going to sound crazy before I even said it. "Yeah, but that new guy I told you about—they gave it to him."

She gave a low, bitter chuckle. Her shoulders jerked up like she couldn't decide if she wanted to laugh or cry.

"So, you got overlooked again, huh? And what makes you think this one deal will make things different?"

"Because John chose *me*," I said, sticking my chest out a little. "They know the new guy can't handle this."

Now she let out an obvious laugh. A pity one. "So, you come home every day bragging about being the best this and the best that but it's still not enough to get noticed? Micah, you put all your trust in a company that doesn't even care about you."

"Regina," I sighed, putting a hand on her shoulder. "You don't understand how the corporate world works. You gotta keep grinding to prove yourself."

"Well… at least you'll prove your worth to someone."

She got up from the couch and headed for the kitchen. She always did that in moments like this—say something then walk away before I could respond. How does she expect to fix things if she never wants to finish them?"

"Regina, can you come back in here so we can finish this conversation?"

She kept walking. "The sink's dripping again, Micah. Somebody's gotta fix it."

"I'll get it."

But she didn't stop—just kept walking like I hadn't said a word.

I got up and followed her. I immediately saw a puddle of water spreading beneath the cabinet, a mess waiting on top of the mess we were already in.

Regina got down on her knees and tried to tighten something with her bare hands.

"Regina," I said, crouching next to her. "Hold on—let me go shut off the water first."

I rushed to the garage and shut the valve, then came back inside with fresh towels and dropped to my knees beside her. She was still trying to twist at the pipe with a towel wrapped around her palm.

"Here, let me do it."

"I got it," she shot back.

"No, let me."

She shoved the towel in my hands. "Fine. Fix it. You were supposed to do it two weeks ago but go ahead now. Always want to do something when I'm forced to handle it myself."

I let out a slow breath, trying not to snap. "It wasn't that bad then."

"Do you always have to wait until things get bad before you decide to step up?"

There was more to read between the lines, but I decided to let it go. Regina was just frustrated and saying something would only make it worse.

"I'm going to fix it in the morning," I said softly. "The store is closed right now."

"Seems like you have a lot to do tomorrow. I don't want to add to your busy schedule."

I didn't respond. I just grabbed the towels and soaked up as much water as I could. I made a mental note to get up early, check a few emails then run to the store to get the part.

Later that night, we got in bed without saying

much to each other. I laid on my side, watching the ceiling, trying to find the right time to reach for her. When I finally did, she barely moved.

"I'm tired," she whispered, and turned away.

I stayed there, arm half-extended, breathing in the space where closeness used to be.

Minutes later, she was asleep. Or pretending to be.

Either way, I was alone.

We drove separate cars to the school. My bag was already packed and in the trunk. I double-checked my flight time before pulling out of the driveway. 2:06 PM. I prayed that the ceremony would go quickly and smoothly so I could be out of there no later than noon.

The parking lot was almost full when I arrived. I spotted Regina's car and parked close to it.

She was seated near the front with a few of the other parents, laughing at something one of them said. When she saw me approaching, she scooted over and gave a polite, yet seemingly forced smile.

"Hey," I said.

"Hey," she replied, eyes still on her friend, smiling harder than normal.

The woman next to her leaned forward and extended her hand out to me. "You must be Micah. I've heard so much about you. I'm Courtney."

"Nice to meet you," I said, then looked at Regina who was still avoiding eye contact. "Hopefully it was all good things."

Courtney and I made small talk for a few seconds while Regina sat between us like a robot. Or a tired pet, waiting for me to shut up.

Once we wrapped up, I leaned closer, our thighs pressed up against each other. I waited a second to see if she'd move over. When she didn't, I took it as if she was feeling a little better.

"Want some coffee?" I asked. "They have some up front."

"I'm good."

And just like that, she turned toward Courtney and started talking to her again. A few other moms joined in. I tried adding my two cents but it felt awkward every time. Regina was giving me one-word answers without even looking my way.

I honestly didn't get why she was reacting this way. I understood the trip had her heated, but didn't I at least deserve some credit for showing up today? Nearly every seat was filled with moms. Where were all the dads?

Regina didn't appreciate me the way a wife should. I busted my butt to give her a life we never had—killing myself at a job she never stops complaining about.

But I shifted my attention when music started playing over the speakers.

I placed my arm around her shoulder. "Think they're about to start?"

"I don't know. But if you need to leave now, you can."

I moved my arm quickly. *See?* I try, but she always has an attitude.

I leaned in, dropping my voice to that low tone you use with a rebellious kid who acts out in public. "What's wrong with you? I can't ask a simple question?"

She ignored me.

My phone vibrated and I pulled it out of my pocket. A text from John.

John: Thanks for taking this trip! The meeting's set up for 11 a.m. sharp but please be get there as early as possible. I just found out they're meeting with one of our competitors right after us so we want to get in there and impress them before they even meet with them.

I smiled, feeling a little more confident.

Me: Np John! Lisa put me in a hotel right next to their office so I see no issues with getting there on time.

John: Good. If you run into any trouble, feel free to reach out. But I'm sure you won't. You got this!

I loved his message. John had nothing to worry about. I knew what I was doing. I'd been in these kinds of situations plenty of times before.

I pulled up some info on the client, making sure I knew exactly what they needed. They were a large firm, looking for longevity and good rates—something we could offer.

The noise around me faded as I scrolled, my focus narrowing in. After a few minutes, I glanced up from my phone. Still no sign of Xavier's class.

On instinct, I opened my maps app. Traffic was already backed up.

I leaned toward Regina, urgent but careful. "Hey, if he's not out in ten minutes, I may have to leave."

She didn't even look at me. "Do what you gotta do."

I swallowed down my frustration and waited. Five minutes. Then another five.

A kid gave a speech—cute, inspirational. Then the principal walked on stage for what sounded like an intermission. That was it.

I touched Regina on the thigh. She kept her eyes straight ahead. She already knew what I was about to do. I kissed her anyway.

"Tell Zay I'm proud of him. I'll see you guys on Friday. Love you."

She stuck her hand up, somewhere between a wave and a dismissal.

But I had no time to argue. Besides, I was still keeping the faith that things would get better. I'll have to tell John no more last-minute trips. And speaking of trips… we needed one. Not just any trip but a trip to see our family in Jacksonville.

I'll book it this weekend.

Just as I made it to the exit, I saw a line of students coming out from the side. Xavier was near the end. My heart jumped.

I waved at him.

He waved back, but it wasn't the excited, bright-eyed wave I was used to. It was small. Nonchalant. Like he was glad I showed up, but also knew I was leaving.

I stood there for a second. Wanting to say something but couldn't think of any words. Nothing I'd said made a difference to Regina, I knew it wouldn't to him either.

I left. Drowned in my thoughts. Couldn't even have the airport excitement I'd always get.

Halfway there, it started raining. Light at first, but by the time I got there, it was pouring.

The airport doors slid open and I stepped into a different kind of chaos. Families bunched together, business travelers in a hurry. Security felt longer than usual. Shoes off, belt off, laptop out, pockets empty. It felt like another process I had to pass through to prove myself.

I barely glanced at the signs as I made my way toward Gate 13. I was focused. Wanted to get this over with so I can come back home to my family and make it up to them.

But when I got to my gate, I saw something that every traveler hates to see.

Flight 132: DELAYED.

I walked over to the agent's counter, catching the end of her conversation with the person ahead of me. I held on to a sliver of hope that maybe she'd tell me something different.

"Hey," I said, flashing a polite smile once she looked up at me. "Any update on Jordan Heights?"

She shook her head, apologetic. "Not yet. The weather's still pretty bad so it could be a while."

"You think they'll cancel the flight?"

"I can't say either way. Sorry."

I exhaled slowly, feeling the knot in my chest tighten. "Any other flights going out tonight?"

"No, this is the last one."

I knew that already. But I was hoping she'd mention a connecting flight or something. But no—she just kept it straight forward, already making eye contact with the person behind me.

"So, what am I supposed to do? Just sit and hope this plane leaves tonight?"

Her expression tightened. "Sorry, but at this time, I have no other updates. Please, just be patient. We'll make an announcement as we know more."

Normally, I'd thank the person and walk away, but with everything at stake, I didn't want to risk it. Besides, this airline was notorious for cancelations.

"What about the morning flight?" I pressed. "If this flight doesn't leave can you assure me that I can get on that one?"

"Are you a rewards member?"

"No. If I was paying for this flight myself, I'd never choose you guys."

Her shoulders lifted in a tired shrug. "Well, sir, I can only put rewards members on standby."

My eyelids crinkled. "That doesn't make any sense. So, if this flight gets canceled, what's gonna happen to the rest of us?"

She sighed, waving the next person forward before giving me one last look.

"Sir, if that happens, we'll make an announcement and get everyone rebooked."

The woman behind me stepped up. I moved to the side, curious to see what the agent would say to her. It wasn't normal for me to eavesdrop, but something pulled me in that I couldn't explain. Maybe it was the tension in the air, or maybe I was just desperate for any piece of information.

The woman asked about her flight status, and the agent gave her the same answer she'd just given me. Then, with a hopeful tone, the woman asked, "Is there any chance I can get on standby for the next flight? I'm a rewards member."

The agent nodded, polite but firm. "Name?"

"Naomi Parker," the woman replied smoothly.

I watched as the agent typed her name into the system and guaranteed her standby if the flight gets canceled.

As she was walking away, I realized I was holding my breath a little. It wasn't attraction—but something about the moment—the way our eyes briefly met as she waited felt significant. Like a silent acknowledgment passed between us, even though we were strangers.

"Hey," I said, offering a smile. "So, being a rewards member comes with all those perks, huh?"

She chuckled, a little dry. "Yeah, perks—if you call them that. This airline still sucks."

I smiled. "Fair enough. Micah, by the way."

"Naomi."

We fell into an odd silence. She looked around like she was trying to decide if she should say something. Finally, she leaned in a bit.

"Listen, would you mind walking back over to my seat with me—just until I feel safe? There's this older gentleman who kept staring at me then all of a sudden came and sat by me. It's kinda creepy."

I hesitated. It felt... off. Then I noticed the ring on her finger. *Maybe she just wasn't used to flying alone.*

I followed her gaze, scanning the crowd, but saw nothing or no one strange.

She looked also and shook her head. "Never mind. Maybe he was a janitor on break or something."

"So, you're good?"

She gave a small, bashful smile. "Yeah, I'm good. Thanks. Have a nice day."

I returned the smile. "You too."

As soon as she walked off, reality hit again. I needed to figure out something. I walked back toward the seating area and called John. He answered on the first ring.

"Hey, Micah."

"Hey," I said, shoving my free hand in my pants pocket. "They're saying my flight is delayed and might even get canceled."

He let out a sharp breath. "See, Micah, this is why I wanted you to take the early flight. There's no one else that can get there in time. If this deal doesn't happen—"

"It will happen," I interrupted. "I'll figure it out."

"How?" he countered. "I don't think you'd be calling me if you knew what to do."

"I do," I said, a thought popping in my head. "I just wanted to make you aware of the situation."

"Well, thanks," he said, his voice dripping with sarcasm. "Keep me posted."

"Okay."

I hung up, clenching the phone in my hand, staring at the long line that had now formed. There was no point in getting back in line. There was no point in sitting either, just to get hit with a cancellation. I had to decide myself on what to do.

I pulled out my phone and searched, Dallas to Jordan Heights.

An eight-hour, seventeen-minute drive.

I could drive that easily. If I left now, I'd get there just before ten. I'd done trips from Jacksonville to Norfolk back when Regina's sister was in the military.

This drive was similar.

I'll do it.

I called Regina to tell her but she didn't answer. Figured she wouldn't. I left a voicemail. Then left the airport quickly.

Jordan Heights… I'll be there. And on time.

CHAPTER TEN

Jordan Heights… There was no chance I could make it on time.

At least not with these barricades in my way.

I thought about moving them, but there were too many. Plus, who knew what kind of danger might lie ahead if I forced my way through.

Might not even be the right way. The GPS clearly didn't know this was there. Too risky.

I should just turn around. Drive until I see that first Jordan Heights sign.

Or maybe just go home and try to patch things up with Regina.

I thought about it—It was 10:54. I was still in the same clothes from yesterday, with no clue where this place even was. And even if I called to tell them I was running late, what was I supposed to say? I didn't have an ETA—or anything solid I could give them.

I was tired. Tired of running from what mattered most and wasting myself on what meant nothing. To this client, I was just a potential business partner. But to my family, I was everything—and I'd been too blind to see it. Running on fumes for years. Chasing praise like it was coffee—just enough to keep me awake, but never enough to keep me whole.

I gave the barricades one final look. I knew it wasn't going to do me any good just standing here.

I turned around, looking at the road behind me. The way I'd come. I thought about all the high hopes I'd had starting out but they were long gone.

And now I had to retrace my steps—go back the way I came.

I walked back to the car, got in and bowed my head.

"God, I don't even know where I'm at or what lies ahead. But You do. So please... guide me. If I've been chasing the wrong things, please redirect me. If I've drifted too far, please pull me back. Help me. But please don't leave me. I want to fix my life."

"Even if it hurts. Even if I have to suffer for a while."

"In Jesus's name. Amen."

When I opened my eyes, it was like my words pressed down on me. I finally saw the truth I'd been dodging for years.

I had been so focused on closing deals that I didn't notice doors closing behind me. Chances to make things right with Regina. But I failed her. And maybe I'd never get her trust back.

She tried to leave me once before—years ago, when Xavier was a toddler. That time, I talked her down. Promised her I'd be better. But all I did was got real good at apologizing but not so good at changing.

This time felt real. I didn't hear the fight in her voice—just release. Like she'd already let go in her heart and was just waiting for her mind to catch up.

I exhaled and shrugged. I'd already prayed. Now I had to let go and let God deal with it. Maybe it was too late to patch things up. Maybe not.

I started the car and turned around. I didn't have a determined direction. Just knew I needed to go back this way.

The road curved gently, giving me a sense of familiarity. I started seeing small details that I missed earlier.

Then I thought about Lior.

He wasn't here now, but somehow, his words still echoed in my head. He hadn't forced anything on me. He didn't guilt-trip, didn't preach. He just asked questions I didn't want to answer.

He saw the pattern of my life after only a few hours in the car with me. The slow, quiet way I'd let life pass by while I stayed busy chasing the next title, the next bonus, the next reason to stay disconnected.

Regina followed me to three different cities over the past ten years. Left her friends, her family, her church, her mother. All because I said, 'This job will be better for us. This move is the one.' I convinced her that moving meant growth. That every time we packed boxes, we were building something stronger.

But now I wonder if we've just been relocating our problems. Shifting our environment but neglecting our mindset.

Regina never wanted to leave home. She said she

liked being near family. Even though they got on her nerves sometimes, we could have moved across town. But she followed me anyway. Each time with more faith than I had in myself.

I guess I confused sacrifice with avoidance. Thinking I could just stay busy and not deal with the issues. Thought money could buy love—or at least mask it.

When Lior asked, 'Is she happy? Is she lonely?' I brushed him off. Got defensive. Told him he didn't get it. That when you have a family depending on you, rest isn't an option.

But maybe he understood better than I did. Maybe he'd seen someone else crash doing the same thing. Or maybe he was sent. That none of this was a coincidence. I was meant to stop at that diner yesterday. I was meant to see him.

But if that's true, I blew it. I blew everything. Lior was gone. My job probably was too.

And my wife.

I'll just have myself and my selfish ways.

I cried out to God again. *"Lord, wherever this road leads next—I'm asking You now… Please let it be somewhere I still have something waiting for me. Even if it's just You. That's all I need."*

Keep going.

The voice wasn't loud—just a nudge deep in my spirit. His presence settled over me, giving me patience and peace.

But even with that quiet peaceful voice, I still

heard the loud ones too. The ones saying, *you're wasting time. Turn around! Force yourself through that barricade! That's the only way!*

Normally, I'd listen to those voices. I'd let the pressure win. Push forward with pride even when the path was partially blocked. I'd call it ambition, call it drive, call it making myself happy… and since God allowed it, He was okay with it.

But this time, the road *was* blocked. And I still wasted time trying to find a way through. Following my GPS when I should've been following his.

God's Planned Steps.

I took a deep breath, kept my hands on the wheel. Thought about a verse I'd heard it a while back.

"So do not throw away your confidence; it will be richly rewarded. You need to persevere so that when you have done the will of God, you will receive what He has promised."

That's it. I didn't need to force my way into a blessing that He hadn't sent. I didn't need to earn something He'd already called me to inherit. I just needed to stay faithful—and let obedience speak louder than urgency.

But why didn't these verses pop up yesterday before I left the award ceremony? I wouldn't have even taken this trip.

I drove for ten more minutes. And out of nowhere, a billboard appeared. Faded, but somehow clear as day.

"Your Destiny Is Ahead — Keep Driving!"

It was for an old theme park, probably long shut

down. The picture showed a smiling family in front of a roller coaster, with the little kid pointing toward it like he couldn't wait to get on. He was full of joy. No stress. No hesitation.

I stared at it until it slipped past.

That kid knew the ride would have dips, curves, twist and turns, but he was still excited.

Maybe that was the point.

Keep going even though I didn't know what lied ahead. Smile. Get excited again. Life will have bumps, but trust that God will always be there.

Soon, the road dipped into a valley, then opened wide into a town that looked like every other place I'd passed—brick storefronts, quiet streets, trees lining the sidewalks.

Something about it carried the same feeling as last night.

Then I saw something.

A small diner. Plain. Nothing flashy. Just a dusty sign in the window that read OPEN and a few cars parked out front.

And just like before—something told me to stop.

So, I did. Pulled in, gave the place a quick scan. But the second I opened my door, I froze.

No way.

This wasn't even the same place I dropped him off at!

He stood there. Same calm posture. Same stare. Standing near a bench like he'd been waiting all along. Like he knew I'd show up.

Was I dreaming? Did he follow me? Did someone bring him here and this was another coincidence?

Or was it all a part of the plan?

His plan? Or *His* plan?

I didn't know what to think. All I knew was that this was something I couldn't run from this time.

I got out and headed toward him. Slow at first, then faster.

When I reached him, I was at a loss for words. I just wrapped my arms around him.

And he didn't resist.

We stood there, me clinging to him like a lifeline.

Finally, I pulled back, keeping my hands on his shoulders.

"How… how did you get here?" My breath was short and shaky.

Lior smiled, tilted his head like he expected that question.

"Sometimes it's not about *how* you get there… but why."

I let out a laugh, shaking my head. There he goes again. But this time, I embraced it.

"Listen," I said, sliding my hands off his shoulders and into my pockets. "I'm sorry about earlier. I wasn't thinking straight. If you need a ride anywhere, I got you. Seriously."

He smiled, softer this time. "Micah, no need to apologize. You weren't wrong for trying to get somewhere, you just forgot that arriving doesn't change you. The journey does."

I stood there, his words hitting me slow and

deep. He was right. I hadn't reached my destination, but the ride did change my perspective.

"I'm just tired, man," I finally admitted. "Tired of messing everything up. I don't even know if I have enough time to fix things."

Lior stepped off the curb and started walking toward my car.

"Then stop wasting whatever time you think you have," he said over his shoulder. "Come on."

He didn't even look back. Just kept walking.

And I followed.

CHAPTER ELEVEN

I pulled the sun visor down as I started the ignition. The sun was bright—brighter than it had been all morning. I checked the time. 11:46 A.M.

Still, I felt lighter. Seeing Lior again felt like finding the one familiar thing in a strange place. I was thankful I had a chance to restart this journey with him.

I turned to him as I put the car in drive. "Which way are we headed?"

He gazed out the window, looking behind him. "Let's go that way."

I pulled out slowly and eased onto the road. Soon, the sun started slipping behind the clouds, leaving me with a clear view ahead.

I was about to ask him where we were headed, but I caught myself. Part of me still wanted control, but another part knew I didn't need it.

For a while, it worked. Ten minutes of straight highway, only thinking about how happy I was to have him back in the car with me.

But then another question popped up. One I couldn't ignore.

"Alright, Lior," I said. "What's really going on here? Everything that's happened today and yesterday—none of it feels random. Even if you don't have every detail, I need to know I'm not tripping and this isn't just some coincidence."

He gave a knowing smile. "No, you're not losing your mind, Micah. Sometimes this is how it feels when God starts moving quickly in your life. You prayed for direction—but that doesn't mean it comes as clear as you want it."

I nodded, then told him about the argument I had with Regina shortly after dropping him off. Not the play-by-play, just the weight of it. The distance in her voice, the way it felt less like a fight but more like a final goodbye.

"I think she's done with me," I admitted. "I've screwed up more times than I can count. Ignored all her cries. The silent ones and loud ones."

Lior looked at me evenly. "If she is done, do you think it's because of your mistakes… or because you stopped trying?"

I looked at him for as long as I could, but the road started to curve and forced me to split my focus. I didn't know how to answer his question—and I think he knew that. He wasn't waiting on a response anyway. He just wanted me to reflect.

There was a time I used to care—used to try harder. I'd plan movie nights, late dinners after the boys went to bed, even little games just to make her laugh. Sometimes I'd even take her phone from her hand just to pull her closer.

But somewhere along the way, I did stop trying. Now I just sit on my side of the couch, watching her scroll for hours, saying nothing. I still want the connection—even if we just sat and talked about random things. But she doesn't give it, and I don't fight for it anymore.

I'd tell myself I was giving her space, but deep down I knew I was just trying to avoid conflict. Keep the peace. Stay quiet. Because any little moment could blow up into something bigger, and I didn't want to fight.

As a result—the space between us grew. I chose to stay busy at work. Over time, she noticed. She'd say things like *we need to spend more time together* or try to spark up random conversations. We did, but it never lasted long. We'd just drift back into our ways, each of us waiting on the other to step up.

For a while, I felt like she was purposely trying to make my life miserable. Why complain that I wasn't home, but when I was, act like she didn't even want to talk to me? The only time I had her full attention was during intimacy.

Lior shifted in his seat and I turned to him. The way his eyes met mine—it was unsettling, like he wasn't just reading my mind but placing thoughts in my head.

And that's when it hit me. A conviction I couldn't shake. Maybe I'd been pointing in the wrong direction this whole time. Maybe I should've been looking at myself first.

I stopped leading. I let work, frustration, and pride set the pace, and in the process, I drifted. Regina wasn't asking for the world—she just wanted balance. To feel seen. To know her voice mattered in our marriage, not just in the moments when she threatened to leave.

She wanted to feel chosen every day, not only when I needed her. To know I desired her, not just depended on her. And the more I thought about it, the clearer it became—I hadn't given her that in a long time.

She deserved more credit than I ever gave her. She held our family together through storms I barely acknowledged. She still prayed over me when I didn't even have the words for myself. Even in her anger, she was fighting for us, not against me. I just hadn't seen it.

Lior cut through my thoughts.

"What do you think her main problem is with you working so much?"

I froze for a moment. Not because I didn't know, but because I suddenly did. It was like God slipped the answer right inside me—as if He knew I was now ready to face it.

"It's not the work," I said slowly. "It's that I treat her like a business. She handles the house, I handle the income… and somewhere in all that, I stopped making her feel loved. It's been all technique and no tenderness. All logistics but no love."

Lior grinned but tried to clean it up before I

looked over at him.

"At what point did it shift from love to this new version?"

"I can't say when, but I definitely know why. I've always had this fear of being broke like we were when I was growing up." I let out a small chuckle. "Man, I remember one Christmas Eve—I must've been six or seven, my uncle showed up at our house with bags of toys for us since my dad didn't have any money left over. I was grateful, but something about it stuck with me and I never wanted to put my family in a spot where we had to depend on someone else."

Lior nodded slowly. "So, you made a vow. Somewhere in all that pain, you told yourself that you'll never feel like that again."

"Yeah, I guess I did."

"And now you measure love in paychecks."

I shrugged. "I wouldn't say that. I just know how money—or lack thereof, can make a kid feel. All your friends have things but you don't."

"But do they have love?"

I didn't answer. Lior placed his arm on the middle console. "Micah, love isn't measured by money. It's measured by intentional presence. Being there for your kids will take them further than money ever could."

"I hear you, Lior," I said, shifting in my seat. "My dad loved us—was always there for us. But we were broke. Why wasn't I happy then?"

"Because love doesn't cancel reality," he said, voice calm but steady. "It doesn't erase the pain of an empty fridge or worn-out shoes. But it *does* show up in the middle of it."

After a pause, he continued. "Your dad's love didn't fix the money problems—but maybe it held your family together when everything else was falling apart. Love's not a replacement for provision. It's the reason you keep showing up, even when provision's not there yet."

His words pressed on me—gentle, but undeniable.

I still had questions, though. Not out of aggression, but growth.

"But why did God let us go through that?"

Lior let out a chuckle. "That's the million-dollar question, ain't it? Sometimes, God lets us *feel* the lack so we'll learn where the true supply comes from. Not to punish—but to prepare."

He tapped the dashboard lightly.

"You didn't just survive that season—you *became* something in it. And maybe the pain you felt as a kid is the same pain that's making you a better father now. God doesn't waste anything—not even struggles."

I swallowed hard, the weight of it sitting in my chest. "You might be right," I muttered. "But am I wrong for wanting different for my family?"

"Not at all. Wanting different ain't wrong, Micah. It's human. It's love. But *different* doesn't always mean *better*. Your dad left behind bills, yeah... but seems like he also left behind a blueprint of resilience. Of how to love through lack. Now it's your turn to add to that."

Tears began to roll down my face. I knew Lior didn't have all the answers, but everything that I was holding in, was starting to rise to the surface. Things I was too scared to ask because people said *never question God.*

Yet somehow, with Lior, it felt different. He made space for my questions. Helped me see the difference between questioning and challenging God.

"But what about my dad?" I asked. "Was that his destiny? Just to live a poor life to teach us?"

Lior raised his chin. "Truth is—I can't answer that. But what I can say is that God knows the full story. He might've died with little money, but from what you told me, he had a big heart. He left behind more than bills. He left impressions. Look at how you love your kids. You want them to be happy, just like your dad wanted you to be. You turned out to be a good man, Micah. So, I think he died proud."

I stared out the windshield, letting that sink in.

"I don't know about being a good man," I said. "My dad would never choose a job before us. Matter of fact, I don't even know what I should do about my job. That's if I even have one."

Lior gave a soft chuckle, not mocking—just honest.

"Just pray, pause and listen. Ask God what's next instead of assuming. I can tell you one thing—this isn't about throwing everything away and starting over. It's about shifting your reason *why*. Work isn't the enemy, Micah. But when it becomes your identity—your refuge, your worth—then yeah, something has to give."

Everything that came out his mouth was truth. Things I already knew—but somehow didn't see it clearly until now.

I had a lot in my life that needed to be fixed.

My work ethic.

My childhood trauma.

My marriage.

Regina's voice echoed in my head—not the words, but the pain behind them. The tired edge, the release I heard when she spoke like she'd already let go but was still trying to protect my feelings.

I took a deep breath. "So, what about my wife?" I asked. "After all this… clarity I just had, what if she still wants to leave?"

Lior spoke quickly. "You love her anyway. Not because it's easy. But because *you* made a vow."

"But what if it makes me look like a fool?"

He chuckled again. "Love is unconditional. Let her walk if she needs to—but don't close the door on your end. You don't chase her… but you don't harden either. Realize where you went wrong and stay soft enough for God to speak through you. And when the time comes to reconcile, you'll know it."

I switched hands on the wheel, letting the other rest on my thigh. "I just hope she can see the change in me before it's too late."

"Maybe she will. And maybe she will and won't fully trust it. Just plant the seeds. Let your change speak louder than your need to be with her."

I stared at the road for a moment, quiet. Then I whispered, "You're right. But I'm just afraid that no matter what I do, she's gonna think I'm the same person I was before. And I don't trust how I'll react."

"Then be honest with God about that, Micah. Tell Him you're scared. Tell Him you don't trust yourself. That's not weakness—that's wisdom. You don't have to fake strength. You just gotta stay surrendered. If you try to prove you've changed, you'll fall right back into the old patterns. But if you *walk* in the change—quietly, daily, faithfully, God will make sure it takes root in you. And if she's planted too, then in time, those roots will grow toward each other again."

His words settled over me, heavy but steady. Part of me wanted to just take it, believe it, let the weight lift. But another part kept pushing back—stubborn and restless.

Could it really be that simple—just surrender and trust?

I exhaled, slow and shaky. "Lior, I have no doubt you are speaking truth. But am I wrong for really wanting my marriage to work? I admit, some of it is pride. No one in my immediate family has gotten a divorce and I don't want to be the first."

Lior shook his head. "Micah, you can't carry your whole bloodline on your back. That's not your job—it's God's. You're not failing your family by releasing what you can't control. You're honoring them by choosing faith when it hurts the most."

I sat with his words, letting them echo longer

than I wanted. But deep down, it was truth. The more I replayed it, the more it pressed on me—not as a demand, but as a seed being placed in soil I didn't even realize was ready.

Choosing faith.

God had a bigger plan. Maybe this wasn't about saving my marriage. Maybe it was about saving me.

My voice dropped lower, but more certain. "You know… maybe God's been stripping all this away so I'd finally stop performing and just be who He's called me to be. For real this time."

Lior smiled, leaning back into his seat. "That's a good way to see it."

I stuck my chest out. "Yeah… I'm not perfect— I don't have to be. I just have to live the life I was called to."

I now felt steady. Less on edge. Everything Lior said, seemed as if it was coming straight from God.

We rode in silence for a while and suddenly the road narrowed. Then it opened into a familiar sight.

The place where I'd turned around.

The dead end. The barricades still there.

I eased my foot off the gas and brought the car to a stop.

"This is where I turned around," I said, pointing out the windshield. "Right here. Now what do we do?"

Lior leaned forward, squinting. "Do you see that little path right there?"

I looked. "No. Where?"

He pointed again, sharper this time. "Look a little

more to the right."

I leaned over the wheel, following the angle of his finger. Just to the side of the main road, barely noticeable was a narrow dirt trail.

"How was I supposed to see that?"

Lior grinned. "You weren't. You were never meant to be on this road alone."

CHAPTER TWELVE

For the past hour or so, I felt like a sponge, soaking up Lior's wise words. Truth after truth, laid out without judgement. He might not have known it, but he was helping me find the language for my problems. Things I couldn't say or interpret, he was right there to guide me through.

He paused between thoughts so I could feel what he was saying, not just hear it. I started seeing things clearer. Bad patterns, pride, selfishness and disbelief that things would ever get better.

The good thing is that Lior didn't offer fixes for my situations. He just kept pointing me back to the Holy Spirit. I could chase a thousand ways to improve my situation, but without God, none of it would hold. Only what's built on Him stands.

"Micah, can I ask you something else?" he asked, after a few minutes of silence. "If someone were to ask you if you really love Jesus, could you say yes and be one hundred percent sure that you do?"

At first, I thought it was a simple question—almost too simple. The answer felt obvious, but I still hesitated, turning it over in my head. When I looked at Lior, though, he wasn't staring me down or making it feel like a test. He was calm, almost inviting, like he'd wait as long as it took for me to see it on my own.

"I think so," I finally said. "My life doesn't always line up like I love Him, but I'm trying to get there."

Lior gave a nod like he was satisfied with that answer but still had more to draw out of me.

"Now, let me ask you this… do you think his discipline means He's mad at you?"

My mind immediately went back, sifting through years of striving. Times I pushed past every warning sign. Times I made moves without prayer, too busy chasing the next thing to stop and listen. Nights I stayed late at work, drowning out conviction in the name of providing. Regina's voice echoing in my memory—pleading, warning—all while I brushed her off. Too many moments to name, each one stacking up like evidence against me.

"Yeah," I said quietly. "I've been doing my own thing for years. Maybe this is Him sitting me down— making me face it. Maybe this is discipline, I guess."

Lior breathed slow through his nose as if he was trying to stay grounded. His face shifted slightly— somewhere between contentment and concern, like he was grateful I'd said something, but not quite settled with the answer.

Without a word, he reached for that old bag he'd been carrying. He unzipped it and pulled out the small Bible. He flipped toward the back of it and skimmed quietly, nodding to himself as he landed on something.

Then he looked up at me.

"Would you say it's a big deal for us to pay attention to His discipline?"

I adjusted my posture and nodded. "Of course."

"Why?"

I hesitated, leaning into a pause. Was this supposed to be obvious? Or maybe one of those spiritual pop quizzes where the answer was simpler than I wanted to make it.

"Maybe so we can change our ways," I answered. "Stop making the same mistakes."

Lior tilted his head. "And then what? Make new mistakes?"

I let out a quiet chuckle. I really didn't know what to say. He knew it too, and he didn't press me for an answer. Instead, he just picked his Bible back up.

"It's more than just messing up, Micah. It's about growth. Hebrews 12 tells us that His discipline produces something—a harvest of righteousness and peace for those who've been trained by it."

He took a breath and continued. "Discipline doesn't feel good. God knows it doesn't. The Bible flat-out calls it painful. But don't go through life mistaking discipline for punishment."

I thought back to all the times I'd taken setbacks as God being angry with me. The closed doors. The jobs I lost. The constant tension in my marriage. Every time, I felt like I was paying for something.

"How do I know the difference?"

"Simple," he said. "Punishment is about paying back what you've done. Discipline is about preparing you for what's ahead. One leaves you feeling like you need to withdraw yourself from God or anyone else because they're mad at you. The other teaches you to draw closer. And yeah—discipline can *feel* like punishment, because our emotions and understanding can sometimes cloud our view. But over time, you'll see the difference."

His words made sense on the surface, but they didn't sit easy.

"But why discipline? Can't God teach us another way? Especially if we now see what we did wrong?"

Lior leaned back, folding his arms.

"You ever seen a good father let his son do whatever he wants without correction?" he asked, then answered himself. "No. A good father will let you feel it for a while. Not because he's cruel, but because he loves you too much to let you destroy yourself. If He takes the pain away too soon, you'll go back to your old ways. Discipline isn't just about stopping bad habits—it's so you can share in His holiness. He has to let you hit that wall, but the beauty is, once you've been trained by it, He'll move that wall out of your way."

A smiled formed without me even meaning for it to. I leaned deeper into the seat, letting the thought turn over in my mind. Maybe it wasn't punishment at all.

Maybe it was preparation.

Lior looked down at the Bible again, his thumb

gently brushing the crease of the page like he didn't want to miss a word.

"There's more in here," he said quietly. His eyes lifted just enough to meet mine. "If you're not disciplined, then you're not really sons."

His look wasn't accusing—just letting the truth hit how it needed to. "Micah, you have to trust that God isn't distant when He disciplines us. That's actually proof He's close. Proof we belong to Him."

I nodded slowly, then faster, like a light came on inside me. For the first time in a long time, I didn't feel like I had to fix everything on my own. I didn't have to earn my way back into God's favor. I was already in His hands. Even with this discipline—well especially with this discipline… I was His.

"I just need to release control." I'd been saying it in my mind, but I actually saying it, and with authority, shifted something.

Lior closed his Bible but kept his hand resting on it. "Micah, I must warn you," he said. "The hardest part about all this is letting other people walk their own road with Him."

Regina.

Yes, this breakthrough and discipline all made sense, but it was for *me*. My conviction. What about her? How could I get her to see the change in me so she can change her own self?

"Lior," I said calmly. "I've told Regina a thousand times that I'd change. How can I really get her to see it this time—and not only that, how can I get her to walk this path with me?"

He was already shaking his head as I spoke. "That's still wanting control, Micah. Your new walk can involve her but sometimes it can't be *with* her. So, live in a way that blesses her, but let your reason be for Him. That's the only way your change will hold."

He leaned back with a quiet exhale as he continued. "God doesn't waste pain. Not a single drop. Even the stuff you'd rather forget—He uses all of it."

I let that soak in. He was right. As bad as I wanted her to see the change, I need to start with God. That way I'll know if I'm doing the right thing.

"Thanks, Lior," I smiled. "Your words have been encouraging. But honestly, it feels like you stirred something that was already in me. And more is being added… I can't explain it. But if I had to, I'd simply say someone's in the background filling in the rest."

Lior grinned, lifting both hands like a coach in the locker room. "Just think of this as your workout season. You already had the strength and the muscle underneath, just had to get rid of the bad stuff."

I looked down at my stomach, grinning. "So, what are you trying to say, I need to work out too?"

He chuckled. "I'm just saying that the outside will catch up to what God's doing on the inside. But if you want to do a few push-ups, I won't stop you."

I let out a laugh. The kind I hadn't felt in weeks. Maybe longer.

"You know, Lior—you alright with me, man. I still don't know where you came from, but I'm glad you did."

He laced his fingers behind his head and leaned

back. "Appreciate that. I take compliments in words or food, just so you know."

"So, you're hungry?" I asked. "After that big sandwich you ate earlier?"

"I am," he smiled. "Encouragement fills the soul, but food keeps the body going." He paused, then added, "And I'm sure you need something else, too. That milk has probably worn off."

"It did," I sighed, still grinning. "But it was good. You were right, that was all I could probably handle at the time."

He looked out the window. "Something's coming up soon."

We got quiet again. I leaned my head back, letting the rhythm of the road settle me. It was strange how a few hours with Lior felt like weeks of unpacking things I didn't even know were inside of me. It's like finding extra room in a closet that you'd given up on clearing out. But those old shoes, old clothes that you haven't worn in a while—or forcing yourself to fit in… maybe it's time to give them up.

"Funny isn't it?" Lior said with a grin. "The way God steps in, cancels our plans, and sets us up for something better."

"It is," I said. "Two strangers. One car. A whole lot of miles. And somehow, it's exactly what both of us needed."

He winked at me. "Told you we could help each other."

I gave a playful frown, but it gave way to a smile almost instantly.

"Yeah, yeah, you did. And here I thought you were just some weird dude hitchhiking."

He laughed, a full-throated one this time. "Oh, so that's what you thought?"

I lifted my right hand. "Man, I didn't know what to think—not then. But now I know the truth. You're smart. Like really smart."

Lior raised an eyebrow. "Oh yeah?"

"Yep. You should be a pastor. Or better yet—a spiritual GPS or something. You don't preach, you guide people, man."

Lior rubbed his chin, pretending to ponder. "And you? You should be a business owner or something. But good thing I got to know you too because at first, I was thinking you were just some guy who had it all together… but I was wrong."

He let the sentence dangle in the air for a second.

I glanced at him sideways, but smirking. "What do you mean by that? Who am I to you, Mr. Lior?"

He turned toward me with steady eyes. "You're a man who's getting it together. Truth is, none of us have it *all* together, Micah. We're all growing."

I chuckled, thinking about how quiet he'd been most of the day. And now, here he was, cracking jokes while still slipping in wisdom.

"Lior," I said. "Why did you wait so long to open up?"

He kept his gaze straight. "It wasn't my time yet."

I nodded. "So, I guess I need to do the same. Speak my mind only at the right time."

"Something like that. But remember—even Jesus didn't speak in every storm. Sometimes He slept through them."

He stopped for a moment then carried on. "Not every moment calls for words. Sometimes silence is the only space where God can reach us. But today, we had a little bit of everything."

"And I needed it all," I admitted.

Suddenly, his eyes widened as they fixed on an object in the road. Before I could ask what he was looking at, he asked, "Aren't you glad that God hasn't forgotten you, Micah?"

I replied with the first thought that popped up. "You can only forget something if you leave it behind."

For a second, I wondered how he'd respond. But instead of speaking right away, his lips pressed together like he was trying not to smile. The corners gave him away, though. His eyes softened—proud almost, like a father watching his kid finally get it.

"Pull over," he said.

I looked at him, waiting for a smirk or to tell me he was just playing.

Nothing.

His face was steady, looking toward the spot where he wanted me to pull over.

"This part of the road is rough," he followed. "It's best I take the wheel."

I raised an eyebrow. "You sure? You know how to drive right?"

"Just trust me—fully this time."

Something about the way he said it lingered in me, like it meant more than driving. I eased the car to the shoulder, slipped it into park, and stepped out. Once we traded seats, I let my hands fall into my lap. The wheel wasn't mine anymore. Sitting on this side felt different, almost like I'd crossed an invisible line.

My shoulders eased back into the seat. *So, this is what it feels like to not have to drive all day?*

It was strange. I've been behind the wheel so long I forgot there was any other way. I drove everywhere. Planned the route. Never really let Regina drive. Maybe because I didn't trust her to get us there the way I wanted. Or maybe because I didn't know how to let go.

But sitting here, watching the road pass without my hands on the wheel, I realized there's a kind of peace you can't have until you release control. Until you trust that the one driving knows where they're going—even if you don't.

Lior had one hand on the wheel, one resting near the gearshift like he'd been here a thousand times.

The road was indeed bumpy. But he had no hesitation at turns, overcorrections or uneven ground. He anticipated the dips before they came, slowed without braking too hard, drifted wide when potholes appeared.

It seemed like he knew the bends better than the signs did. Just a steady hand guiding us through rough places.

After a few miles, we pulled up to a small restaurant near a canopy of trees. No sign. Just a gravel lot, and a wood exterior.

"Ready to get something to eat?" he asked.

I nodded. "Oh, yeah."

We stepped out and headed inside. The place smelled like butter and cast iron, with old gospel music drifting from hidden speakers. Not many people there—just a couple eating quietly in the corner and a waitress wiping down tables with practiced ease.

We slid into a booth near the window. The waitress came by, handed us menus, and asked what we wanted to drink.

"Water for me," I said.

"Same," Lior replied.

Moments later she returned with our glasses and pulled out her notepad. "Alright, gentlemen, what can I get you to eat?"

I shot Lior a grin. "I don't have to drink milk this time, right?"

Lior gave a faint smile. "No. You're ready for solid food."

We both ordered The Special, which happened to be the same as the other diner.

Once the waitress left, I took a sip of my water and leaned in. "So, let me guess, that milk and solid food line has something to do with Hebrews?"

His brows rose. "Ah, so you know the Bible a little, eh?"

"Not as much as I should."

He shrugged. "You'll get there. Let's just say you've trained yourself for this."

I let out a chuckle. I couldn't explain what he

meant, but somehow… I understood it completely.

Once the food came, we ate quietly. No long speeches. Just good food and enough silence to let everything earlier breathe.

When we finished, Lior paid for the meal then we headed back to the car. I instinctively moved toward the passenger side again.

Lior did too.

"Sorry, my friend. But you're back to driving this last stretch."

I paused, hand on the door handle. "But you were doing fine, man. Way better than I would have."

He nodded. "Exactly. Better than you would have, but now… you're ready."

"Oh, alright," I said with an exaggerated pout then went over to the driver's side. "I see how it is."

Once I got inside, I started the engine and pulled out of the parking lot. The road ahead seemed wider, easier. A few bumps here and there, but nothing like earlier, when everything rattled me.

Or maybe it wasn't the road at all. Maybe it was me. Maybe faith had settled in just enough that the bumps didn't shake me like they used to.

CHAPTER THIRTEEN

For about an hour, we drove in silence.

No directions from Lior. No questions from me. It was like I knew where to turn. Not once did he correct me or point the way.

The silence wasn't empty—it was the kind that lingers when truth has already done its work. When you don't need more conversation because the weight of what's already been said is still speaking.

So, I just drove. Made a few turns when it seemed right, never second-guessing.

Minutes later, my phone buzzed. I glanced down—two bars of service had come back. I hadn't even noticed it was gone until it returned.

A few notifications lit up my screen.

I swiped down. Thirteen missed calls. Twenty-four text messages.

Two voicemails.

John's name showed a few times, then Sean, then the client—and even our office assistant. She never calls unless it's serious.

I hit play on the first voicemail.

John's voice came through, calm but strained. "Micah, it's me, John. Where are you? The client is waiting. Call me as soon as you can."

His tone was sharper on the second voicemail. "Micah, this isn't a good look for you. You're really doing a no call, no show? You better be in a ditch somewhere or have a good excuse. The client decided to pull our offer since they haven't heard from you. See, I knew this was a mistake. You better call me ASAP."

Since my phone was connected via Bluetooth, Lior heard every word.

Normally, my heart would be racing, scrambling for a way to fix it. I'd be writing emails while driving, rehearsing excuses, already halfway to blaming myself for ruining everything.

But this time—none of that. My chest stayed steady. No spiral of guilt, no desperate scramble. Just… stillness. I'd call him when I can.

Because instead of finding Jordan Heights, I found myself.

Found Him.

Lior didn't say a word about the voicemails. He just looked at me. "Micah, tell me about a time you had a big dream. Something you wanted to do but put on the backburner for whatever reason."

My mind sifted through all the moments I once pictured but let fade. Ambitions I put on the shelf. Some were small, others bigger than I'd ever admit out loud.

And then one settled in, solid and sharp.

How did I forget about that one? The one dream that never really left me, even when I buried it under work and excuses.

I turned my head toward him. "Before I started this job, I used to have this vision to open a coffee shop."

He smiled before I even finished the sentence. "Would you say this was a serious vision or just a thought?"

I chuckled. "Oh, no—I had a whole vision board for it. A location, style and all. I even took a barista class just to learn how to make good coffee."

He nodded. "And did Regina support this?"

"Heck yeah," I replied, thinking about everything she did for me. "Regina is the one who found the location for me. Back in our hometown."

"So, what happened?"

"Honestly—life. Bills. I didn't want to put our savings into something that might fail. So, instead I prayed for more income. I started filling out apps and told God if I get a good job first, then I'm going to take it as a sign that He doesn't want me to open it."

Lior went quiet.

I looked over, expecting a thoughtful pause or one of his usual slow nods.

But instead—the corners of his mouth twitched and his shoulders started to bounce.

I shook my head. Here I was thinking that he was giving my comment some deep thought, but all he was doing was holding in a laugh?

I shook my head. "Really Lior? Is it *that* funny?"

He laughed harder. "Sorry, it's just—well, let me get this straight… You asked for something and gave Him the terms and conditions?"

I groaned and laughed with him. "Alright, alright—I know. At least now I do. That was dumb. But that's where I was with life back then."

He nodded then wiped the smile off his face. "I wouldn't call it dumb—many Christians do this. Some don't know how to fully hear His voice so they put terms and conditions on their prayers. *God, if this happens, I'll do this. If You don't do this by this time then that must mean this.* But let me tell you, son—God isn't boxed in by our deadlines or bargains. His word stands on its own."

I nodded slowly as equal parts of conviction and relief hit. I couldn't count how many times I prayed those same bargains. Yet, God was giving me another chance.

I cut my eyes at Lior. "Alright, Lior… I hear you, man. That was deep. But you know what… I miss the old Lior. The one who didn't talk so much. Can you bring him back for a little while. This conviction is serious."

He wiped his face. "Oh, the one you kicked out? Sure." He proceeded to mock his own voice. *"I have a family."*

We both laughed, calming down after a few seconds.

Then his voiced leveled to a more serious tone. "But listen—I want to dig deeper into this. I can feel something here. Tell me, how easy was it to find this job?"

"Not easy at all," I said, shaking my head. "I had to go through three sets of panel interviews—and play the waiting game. All in all, it took about three months to get hired."

"And where was the coffee shop in your mind during the process?"

"It wasn't. After the first interview, I just knew they were going to hire me."

He nodded, mentally registering my replies. "Any regrets?"

A knot rose in my throat. "Yeah. I feel like I missed an opportunity."

Lior leaned in a little. "What kind of coffee shop would you have opened? A small, suburban drive-thru only? Or a big one? Tight space?"

I smiled. "I actually wanted a lounge type. Somewhere where people can converse, work on their laptops, play games, have music soft in the background—and open late."

Lior's face lit up. "That sounds like a great idea. You wouldn't just be selling coffee, you'd be offering presence. Rest for some. A space for people who need to slow down."

I stared out the windshield, letting the image flood my mind. For a moment, it felt close enough to touch.

"Yeah… but it's just a memory now. Regina probably wouldn't want me to open one now anyway."

Lior's voice came gently. "Why not?"

"Because she just laughs anytime I bring it up. She knows my thoughts be all over the place."

"What if she believed you this time? You think she'd support you?"

My eyebrows lifted as I cracked a smile. "Support me? Man, she'd *own* the place. That woman would be all in. Supportive in every way. She knows accounting, knows how to plan and all. She had a vision for everything."

Lior leaned forward slightly, arms folded.

"Then start it."

I blinked and looked over at him. "Start it? Just like that?"

"Yes, just like that."

Something in me lit up. For a second, I could see it—doors open, people coming in, the smell of coffee filling the air.

But almost as quick, the doubts flooded in. This wasn't Jacksonville. This was DFW—higher rent, crowded with strip malls and shopping plazas. I wanted a standalone place, not something crammed between nail salons and dentist offices.

Then, under all the noise, a gentle voice rose in me. It was simple, steady reminding me that maybe Lior was on to something. Maybe I wasn't crazy to believe in it again.

"You really think God will bless me with this?"

"Micah, when God places something in you—something good, something that stirs peace and purpose—you don't bury it just because timing was off. And maybe it wasn't even about time then. Maybe you weren't ready. But hear me—God doesn't throw away what He gives you. Even if you've left it untouched, that vision still lives. So what if you stumble? Who hasn't? The difference is now you're listening. And now—I know you're ready."

"How would that work if Regina—"

"You're ready," he repeated, interrupting the negative thoughts.

I let the words settle in me. This time, I saw it clearer.

Warm light spilling from the ceiling, brick walls wrapping the room in character. Jazz in the background, or maybe some soul instrumentals playing.

Grown folks catching up after work. Books lined across shelves. A chessboard on one table, Bible on another. One group bowed in prayer, while two co-workers chatted a few tables away. Students typing. A couple reading scripture.

It was more than caffeine—it was culture.

I didn't have a name for it yet, but I'd call it something timeless. Not trendy. Something that had faith tied to it. You not only knew it had good coffee, but it also had God.

"Regina always said people needed spaces that weren't just about escaping," I said. "Something to center them. And I remember one time I asked her if she was serious about running it and she looked at me like I was crazy."

Lior nodded, eyes soft. "Then honor that. Start it together. Or start it alone if you have to. But don't keep talking like it's already buried. God didn't kill that vision—you just went a different route. But remember, not every detour is a mistake."

I exhaled and nodded slowly. I didn't have to say anything.

We were in agreement.

And no, I didn't have a new business plan scribbled out. Didn't know how much startup costs would run these days...

But I had the vision.

I could see the people. Hear the voice. And know it's time to do something I was called to do.

"Remember something, Micah. God's not looking for perfect men. He's looking for willing ones. And I'm honored to be on this journey with you."

Those words settled deeper than any sermon I'd ever heard. This drive had stripped me down, layer by layer until all the noise was gone. No titles. No deadlines. No proving. Just a man finally honest enough to stop running.

I didn't have everything figured out. I still had questions. Still had loose ends waiting back home. But for the first time in a long time, I felt ready to face them. Ready to move forward. Not with control. Not with fear. Not to fix my problems. But fix my posture and bring them to God.

With full surrender.

No matter what came next—whether it was fixing my marriage, starting that shop, or facing John— I knew I wasn't walking into it alone.

Lior breathed like he was done. Full. And it seemed like the car itself was carrying the weight of everything we'd been through.

Then something pulled at me. Out the windshield, the shape of a town was rising up.

Something about it made my foot ease off the gas pedal. I slowed down, looking at every house, every building—wondering what about this town had my attention.

Then a flicker on the side of the road. A shape. A shadow. I slowed more, still not sure why. Just had a strong sense of familiarity.

And then I saw it.

The diner!

Same cracked sign. Same old parking lot. Same hotel across the street.

I pulled into the lot without saying a word. My hands steady, my breath catching just a little.

I froze for a moment.

Then Lior touched my shoulder.

"I think this is the end of the road for us," he said quietly. "Mission accomplished. Well done."

I turned slowly to look at him. "Wait... what do you mean?"

He gave me a calm smile. "I think you already know."

Before I could respond, it hit me—like a wave I didn't see coming. All the silence, the questions, the way he seemed to know what I couldn't say out loud. This wasn't just a random ride. It never was.

"Thank you," I said quietly. "Truly, Lior. Thank you."

"No, thank *you*," he said. "None of this would've

happened if you didn't show hospitality to a stranger."

He reached for his bag, zipped it up, and looked at me one last time before getting out. "I'll be thinking about you, Micah. Praying for you."

I nodded, my voice caught somewhere between grateful and undone. "So, where do I go from here?"

Lior didn't hesitate. "I think you know where to go."

Instantly, my phone buzzed in the cupholder. I picked it up and looked at it. The GPS had created a new route itself. No input from me. No voice command. Just a new destination…

Home.

I exhaled. The moment was too divine to question, too ironic to explain. Before I could even put words together, Lior pointed toward the gas pumps. "How about I fill you up one last time? Make sure you have enough fuel to get you home."

I nodded and drove up to the gas pump 2. We stepped out and met near the hood. No words at first. Just a shared understanding between two men who'd traveled further on the inside than the odometer could show.

I stepped forward and pulled him into a hug. Firm and grateful.

"This may sound crazy but I have to ask—will I ever see you again?"

He stepped back just slightly and looked at me. And in that moment, I saw a glow in his eyes. Like something eternal peeking through.

"I believe you will," he said with a wide smile.

"But that'll be a long time from now."

I didn't ask what he meant.

I already knew.

"See you later, Micah. You have all you need now to live a great life the way God intended for you. If life ever gets challenging again, just remember this journey."

I stayed there as he walked toward the diner, his bag over his shoulder, his pace steady and sure.

He didn't look back. He didn't wave. Just disappeared through the glass doors like he'd belonged there.

Moments later, the pump beeped—prepaid for 13 gallons. I filled the tank then climbed back into the driver's seat. I sat still for a moment, then reached for my phone. Opening my messages, I began to type to the one person on my mind:

Heading home.

I hit send.

And started the engine.

Epilogue

The heat pressed down hard. Texas was no stranger to heat, but even for October, this was something else.

I popped the trunk and wiped my forehead with the back of my hand. The bag of fertilizer sat lopsided in the cart like it knew it had no business in this heat.

"This is ridiculous," I muttered. "I shouldn't be doing this."

I had specifically asked Micah to handle it last week. Just like I asked him to fix the sink and the light bulb in the hallway. *"You can get everything from Tool Town on your way home,"* I told him. *"You'll be in and out in ten minutes or less."*

But no. He was too busy. Always had something more important to do.

And here I was—sweat clinging to my back, trying to wrestle a fifty-pound bag into the trunk by myself.

It slipped halfway and thudded to the pavement.

I sighed... loudly.

That's when I heard the voice.

"Let me get that for you."

I turned. A man stood beside me, already lifting the bag with both hands like it weighed nothing. Not too young, not too old. Just… ageless it seems. Normally I could guess anyone's age in a heartbeat, but with him, I couldn't pin it down.

"I'm good," I started, but he was already setting it gently inside.

He dusted his hands and glanced at me. "Fertilizer in triple-digit heat? That's either dedication… or dangerous."

I gave a half-laugh. "Let's try desperation. My grass is dying and my husband didn't have time to do anything about it."

He raised an eyebrow. "Busy with work?"

"Yeah, he's on the road all the time. Sales job."

"I get it," he said. "Let me guess, he's traveling now?"

"Yep. Left yesterday."

Wait. *Why am I telling this man my business?* I get on Micah all the time for talking to random people and look at me doing the same thing.

But honestly, it felt right. There was something about the way he nodded that made me feel seen. Not in the way that only Micah should, but in a way like he understood my pain without me even saying anything.

"How do you feel about that?" he asked.

I drew a blank. "About what?"

"Him being gone all the time."

I wanted to lie like I do to all my friends and family, but it felt like he already knew the truth.

"I hate it," I admitted. "And he knows I do. But yet, my complaining seems to just push him away further. It's breaking me to the point I don't feel like going anymore."

I didn't mean to let all that slip out but I hadn't said anything to anyone else and it felt good getting it off my chest.

"Have you talked to him about this?"

I bristled. "Of course. I'm not the type to keep quiet."

"What does talking to him sound like?"

I stared at him. "Are you stereotyping me?"

"No," he said gently, and didn't crack a smile. "Is it 'I miss you' or 'hey I want to spend time together? Or do you only *talk* when things start to boil over?"

That question didn't land in my ears—it landed in my heart.

I opened my mouth to get defensive but closed it quickly. I knew the truth. My tone was off with Micah almost all the time.

But that's because I've been frustrated for years. Feeling undervalued and unloved.

"Maybe a little bit of everything," I said. "Sometimes I'm angry, sometimes I'm sad… but most times, I don't even care anymore."

He nodded, like he understood more than he let on.

"Well, here's what I can say. A lot of men hear criticism when all they're really craving is connection.

And they don't know how to ask for it, so they just work harder. Provide more. Thinking if they control the narrative, they'll protect everyone."

I looked down at my feet. "But there still has to be a balance, right? And I never told him that he wasn't doing enough."

"Have you ever told him that he is?"

I didn't answer.

This man wasn't accusatory, just honest. Like he was planting seeds I didn't know I needed.

"You ever affirm him?" he followed up. "Not just thanking him for paying bills or mowing the lawn, but really see him? The man behind the role?"

"I used to," I said, quieter now. "When we were younger. Before the promotions. Before the kids. Before… all the moves."

"And all that made you give up?"

I shook my head, although I didn't disagree with his half-question, half-statement.

"Look, I've been pouring into everyone except myself. I'm getting tired, honestly. It's like we're playing this game where he always wins. Always gets his way."

"Do you think he does this *game* on purpose?"

"No. But I do think he only tries to fix things when I pull away. And every time… I just give in— hold it down. Show up for him, the kids, and the house. Move when he wants to relocate… Sorry, I just feel invisible. Like I'm not even allowed to have a voice."

The man didn't jump in right away. He didn't try

to fix it or minimize it. He just looked at me with this steady calm, like someone who'd heard it before… and knew it mattered.

"Sounds like you've been strong for so long," he finally said. "It's like people forgot you were never built to carry it all."

I clenched my jaw to keep from crying.

"Strength is a gift," he continued. "But when it's stretched too thin for too long without rest, it turns into resentment. And when love starts feeling one-sided, it stops being partnership and starts feeling like pressure. Maybe you feel more like a shadow than a partner. Maybe you feel he has you there for convenience rather than love."

My eyes widened. This man spoke like he knew my thoughts.

"You're not selfish for needing space," he went on. "You're tired. You've been pouring into everyone except yourself. And that's not what God intended for you."

I felt the need to say something. Validate his words.

"I just… I don't know how to get him to see it."

He smiled gently. "I think he already *does*."

I blinked. "So, he's doing this on purpose? Manipulating me?"

He shook his head. "I doubt it. You two just have to work together to *express* your feelings. Create a safe space. That's the hard part. Communicating a love the other person can feel."

I shook my head slowly. "But I've tried. I really

have. And when I shut down, he makes me feel like I'm the bad person."

"You're just protecting yourself. That's not a villain. But it *is* fear."

My brows furrowed. "How is it fear?"

"Fear doesn't always get loud. In fact, it hides under silence. Telling you it's safer not to speak than to risk being misunderstood. But that silence can build walls higher than the hurt you're trying to avoid. Walls might keep the pain out... but it also keeps love from getting in."

That hit deep. I thought about the many times I chose to be silent, thinking it was strength. Thinking I was building patience, but really, I was only shutting things out.

And now I felt closed in with no way out.

"So, what do I do?" I asked. "I'm a Christian so God says we can't get a divorce. Not that I really want to, but I don't see how things will ever get better."

I hesitated, but he waited, watching me think, giving me room to go on. "I mean, do I just keep praying, hoping things will change? Or just do something to keep busy?"

"Both," he said, "but not the way you're thinking. Prayer isn't meant to be a hiding place from hard work. So, when you pray, keep showing up as well. And don't just stay busy, stay present. Bring your walls to God one brick at a time and let Him tell you which ones to keep for protection and which ones to tear down for connection. And while you're waiting on Him to move, keep moving in the ways that reflect

His love, even if your husband hasn't caught up yet. Remember, change is easier to believe when it's lived out, not just talked about."

His words sank in, heavier than I expected. For the first time in a long while, I felt something crack open inside me. Finally, hope was pushing through the concrete.

And why did it feel like this man knew me? Knew us?

I tried to make sense of it, but my phone vibrated.

"Well, thank you sir," I said quickly, glancing at my watch. I wanted to keep this conversation going, but it was time to pick up the boys. "But I have to run… it was great talking to you."

"Same to you," he said, grabbing the cart. "Just remember, God just needs you to start. But start with expecting God, not the other person."

He put the cart up, then disappeared around the corner.

Once I got in my car, I checked my phone. A text from Micah. *Heading home.*

I stared at the screen, feeling something I hadn't felt in a long time after hearing those words.

I smiled and typed back, *OK. See you soon. I love you.*

The End

THE SACRED STRANGER

ACKNOWLEDGMENTS

First, thank you, God, for guiding and redirecting my path. You allowed me to stumble upon the book of Hebrews only to press it on my heart to read the entire thing. And now here we are—a novel inspired by it! Thank You for never wasting a detour.

To my wife, Ebone… your love, patience, and presence carry me more than you'll ever know. Thank you for loving me even when life felt like it was pulling us in different directions. Just know that you bring value, strength and beauty into every room you walk into. I see you.

My kids... Thank you for trusting in me to lead you. Thank you for your encouraging words and your excitement about family nights. I am beyond proud of what you're becoming!

To Edgar Butler Jr.— bro eight years ago you and I had conversation about creating books that has changed my life forever! Man, I am blessed to have you as a friend, coach and mentor!

To my One Community Church family, (OCC FAM) I am grateful for your prayers, your support, and your example of what it means to walk in faith.

And last but not least, I want to thank everyone who supported this book, shared a word, or simply believed in me. Thank you. Your encouragement helped bring this to life.

ABOUT THE AUTHOR

Ron Leath is a faith-driven storyteller from Jacksonville, Florida, now living in Dallas, Texas with his wife and two children. A former urban fiction author turned Christian writer, Ron weaves heartfelt, redemptive stories rooted in truth, struggle, and grace.

With titles like *The Sacred Stranger* I and II, his work explores the tension between modern life and timeless faith. Ron writes with a passion to encourage, convict, and remind readers that healing is possible.

When he's not writing, you can find him spending time with his wife, serving at his church, exploring local coffee shops, or cheering on his kids.